## "Maybe I Can Drop By And Tell You A Few Of My Dreams, Doctor...

"If you're intere[...]

Julia couldn't t[...]rt with her. But sh[...] manager would do [...]n performing her job.

"Dream analysis isn't my specialty," she said, trying to ignore the gleam in his eyes that was making her heart skip a beat.

"But it might be fun all the same," he persisted.

Julia was trying to hide the way his warm looks and provocative jokes were unsettling her, but she wasn't sure it was working. Maybe it was the wine, she thought, or the way Storm looked at her with his incredible sexy eyes.

"I guess that depends on what you dream about, Storm."

Dear Reader:

It's summertime, and I hope you've had a chance to relax and enjoy the season. Here to help you is a new man—Mr. August. Meet Joyce Thies's *Mountain Man*. He thinks he's conquered it all by facing Alaska, America's last frontier... but he hasn't met his mail-order bride yet!

Next month will bring a special man from Dixie Browning. Mr. September—Clement Cornelius Barto—is an unusual hero at best, but make no mistake, it's not just *Beginner's Luck* that makes him such a winner.

I hope you've been enjoying our "Year of the Man." From January to December, 1989 is a twelve-month extravaganza at Silhouette Desire. We're spotlighting one book each month with special cover treatment as a tribute to the Silhouette Desire hero—our *Man of the Month*!

Created by your favorite authors, these men are utterly irresistible. Don't let them get away!

Yours,

Isabel Swift
Senior Editor & Editorial Coordinator

# ANNE CAVALIERE
## Squeeze Play

Silhouette Desire

Published by Silhouette Books New York

**America's Publisher of Contemporary Romance**

To those beautiful boys of summer,
the New York Metropolitans

SILHOUETTE BOOKS
300 East 42nd St., New York, N.Y. 10017

ISBN: 0-373-05512-9

First Silhouette Books printing August 1989

Printed in the U.S.A.

**Books by Anne Cavaliere**

Silhouette Desire

*Perfect Timing* #328
*Squeeze Play* #512

---

## *ANNE CAVALIERE*

worked as a reporter in Denver and Minneapolis before turning to writing fiction as a full-time career. She's also held various positions in the field of advertising in New York. Her interests include sailing, antiques and eavesdropping. She presently lives in Seacliff, a small village on the Long Island Sound.

I see great things in baseball. It's our game—the
American game . . . It will repair our losses and be a
blessing to us.

—Walt Whitman

With grateful acknowledgement to Dr. Harvey
Dulberg for his help in researching this book

# One

You're just what my ball club needs, Dr. Archer,"
Charles Granville said. "I have a gut feeling about it."

"Intuition can be a powerful tool," Julia agreed
with a smile. "I've found that most people should
learn to trust those feelings more."

"Damn right." Granville nodded. "You're a psychologist, a professional. You know about these things
from a scientific point of view. Me, I've learned from
experience." Granville dropped three lumps of sugar
into his coffee, then quickly stirred it. The tinkling
sound of sterling silver against fine china made an elegant sort of music, Julia thought. Very fitting for the
hushed atmosphere of his luxurious office. "A smart
fellow puts his money on the horse his gut says will
win. And my bet is riding on you, Doctor."

Although her sleek, dark mane of hair and long legs certainly fit the comparison, Julia could not ever recall being likened to a thoroughbred racehorse. But coming from Charles Granville, she found the remark rather charming.

"It's nice to hear that you have such confidence in my abilities, Mr. Granville. Of course, we will have to discuss the team's problems more before I can agree to work with them."

"Certainly. That's why I've asked Storm Donovan to join us," Granville replied, referring to the baseball team's manager. He pulled an antique gold watch out of his vest pocket to check the time. "If you decide to take on the club, you'll be working very closely with him. He's the best in the business, in my humble opinion," Granville added with a wry smile. "Believe me, I don't blame the man for the slump the team has fallen into this year. Storm has done everything within his power to bring them around. More than any other manager would do, I'll tell you that. Naturally he's taking the situation hard."

"Which is understandable...but his attitude can't be very good for the team's morale," Julia added. From the little she knew about the Boston Eagles, she suspected that the team's loss of confidence and the manager's disappointment were feeding off each other at this point. It was a cycle that was difficult to break, but not inevitably irreversible.

"Very true. Which is why I decided to look outside, for somebody like you—a fresh perspective on the problem. Heck, I considered hypnosis, acupuncture...I even talked with a psychic," he admitted, laughing at himself. "I asked around and heard you were the best. I read about the work you did with that tennis pro...what's his name—"

"Cory Summers?" Julia cut in.

"Summers, right. I noticed on the sports page today that he just won some big tournament in Australia. That's what the Eagles need—a shot in the arm, a kick in the seat of the pants," Granville said heatedly. Julia would have compared her technique of sport performance counseling to something quite different from a "kick in the seat of the pants," but smiling to herself, she didn't interrupt him.

"As for Storm," Granville continued, "these past few years, he's been given free rein with the team. He's built the Eagles up from a last place, nowhere outfit to a championship ball club. He won't be very happy about someone like you moving in on his turf so to speak."

"If I work with the Eagles, I don't plan to move in on anyone's turf," Julia assured him. "I just want the opportunity to work with the players and get things back on the right track. If he is as dedicated to the team as you say, surely he won't object to that kind of help?"

"Let's hope not...but Storm's a proud man. He can be damn bullheaded at times. Part of the reason he's so good at what he does I suppose. Just don't tell me later I didn't warn you."

"I won't, Mr. Granville," Julia promised. To be forewarned is to be forearmed, she thought. But she wasn't alarmed. She had faced Donovan's kind before and probably worse. The manager's resistance to her presence was to be expected. Besides, her professional skills served her well in getting along with the most difficult, even bullheaded, personalities.

"Of course you won't. You're not the type," he said, sounding confident of his own ability to read a person's character. "And enough of this Mr. Granville business," he said good-naturedly. "You call me Charlie. Everybody does."

"Alright, Charlie," Julia nodded, feeling more at ease. Born and bred in sunny Southern California, she was used to a more casual, laid-back style, even at business meetings. She liked Charles Granville and could easily see herself working for him. "Please call me Julia," she told him.

"I will. Lovely name, too," he added taking a sip of his coffee. "Now, let me tell you more about the ball club. We began the season with high hopes of making it to the World Series, Julia. We've got the right stuff. This was going to be the year we'd go all the way." With a shake of his head, he sat back and sighed. "Here we are, at the end of July, losing nine games out of ten."

"Sounds serious," Julia said sympathetically. Had there been any obvious beginning to the team's downhill slide, she wondered. A particularly humiliating loss, perhaps? Or an injury to a key player? A number of questions entered Julia's mind. But for now, she thought it was more important to simply listen to what Charles Granville had to say and learn what she could.

"Bloody right, it's serious. It's a damn embarrassment. Pro ball players, million dollar babies, and they're running around the field like the blasted Keystone Kops." Taking a deep breath, he leaned over to select a cigar from a glossy, mahogany box, which sat beside the silver coffee service. "We can't go on like this," he added in a calmer tone. He lit the cigar, taking a long, thoughtful puff. "Oh, the columnists and other so-called expert so-and-so's already have us dead and buried. But like a guy named Casey Stengel once said, 'It ain't over till it's over.' I'm not giving up on this club," Granville grumbled, puffing away emphatically on his cigar. "No, sir. Not yet. No way, no how."

Julia found Charlie Granville's die-hard belief in his ball club very admirable, even contagious. Hit by a huge blue cloud of cigar smoke however, she could only cough in reply to his stirring speech.

Lost in his own thoughts, Granville didn't seem to notice. The intercom on his desk buzzed sharply and he walked over to pick up his phone. Julia heard him speak briefly with his secretary. Then he hit a button on his phone console, which Julia thought looked like the dashboard of the space shuttle. "Excuse me, a moment. It's our office in Zurich."

"Of course," Julia replied. She sat back, then took a sip of her coffee, glad for a chance to gather her thoughts before the Eagles manager arrived.

She had heard that Charles Leland Granville was eccentric—a multi-millionaire who was more attentive to his baseball team than to running his multinational corporation. Julia disliked hearing people labeled with such commonly misused terms. So far, she liked Charlie Granville very much. He was energetic, down to earth, and direct in his manner and speech. Had she met him under different circumstances, she might never have guessed his powerful position in the business world, or the fact that he was the product of a prominent Beacon Hill family, and a Harvard graduate.

She guessed him to be in the mid-sixties. His small, wiry build, expressive face and silver hair reminded Julia of a leprechaun. A leprechaun in a pin-striped suit accessorized by a bright yellow silk bow tie—one who'd gladly hand over his entire pot of gold to see his baseball team win the World Series.

From their first conversation several weeks ago, Julia could see that at least some of the rumors about Granville were true. Business was not this man's passion. Baseball was—more specifically, the Boston Eagles. An entire oak-paneled wall of Granville's spacious office confirmed that fact. The wall was covered with team memorabilia—photographs, trophies, pennants, autographed baseballs enclosed in glass cases, a framed jersey that bore the name Baxter and the number 25. It was a private collection that Julia thought surely rivaled the exhibits at the Hall of Fame.

He had called her the week before, at her office in San Diego. Their conversation piqued her curiosity about the tycoon. It was important that they meet soon, Granville told her. Every minute counted. Before Julia had even hung up the phone, his secretary was booking a first-class reservation on a flight from San Diego to Boston and a suite at the Ritz Carlton Hotel. Granville's limousine had arrived in front of the hotel at nine o'clock sharp, and had delivered her in sumptuous style to his office.

But it was not Granville's royal treatment that was winning her over. Or even the salary he offered, which was triple her usual fee and admittedly tempting. Julia was most intrigued by the idea of working with a baseball team. Although she hadn't been practicing long, she was already considered a leader in her field. So far, she'd worked mostly with athletes in individual sports: tennis players, golf pros, marathon runners, and even a boxer. Working with an entire baseball team would be quite a change, and a challenge, she thought. Especially with so much riding on the outcome. It would be the perfect opportunity to test out some theories she had about team morale and group attitude.

Though, she suspected working on Donovan's attitude was going to be her first priority. She wondered what Charles Granville had told Donovan about her. Did Granville know that her father was Dan Archer, one of the most famous, well-respected coaches in college sports? Julia was proud of her dad, and he had been a great inspiration to her. She hated it when anyone mistakenly assumed that she had taken advantage of his influence and connections. The Eagles' manager sounded like the type who might.

It had been rough making it in the male-dominated world of professional athletics. Sport performance psychology was a relatively new field, considered controversial by the old guard in the sport world, who were notoriously conservative. Being a woman might have made it doubly difficult to gain acceptance and recognition. Instead, her background had always given her an edge over others in her profession, she thought. She'd virtually been raised on playing fields, and in training rooms. The male chauvinism that might have rattled other women rolled off her back like water. She liked men, and she felt the admiration was mutual. Julia's natural—albeit, traffic-stopping—good looks had been as much of an asset as they were a liability. Experience was key in fending off passes. She was now an expert at making friends. She was dedicated to her work, and she got results. A combination that had earned her the respect of the most die-hard macho-male colleagues.

"Bring on Donovan," Julia silently psyched herself. "Let's see what he's made of."

As if on cue, a sharp knock sounded on the door. "Come in," Granville shouted, momentarily covering the mouthpiece of the phone.

The man on the other side of the door looked in. He was tall, dark and intimidating. It had to be Donovan, she thought, though he was nothing like she had expected. He paused a moment before entering the office, his height and broad shoulders filling the doorway. His gaze quickly swept around the room, finally coming to rest on Julia.

She didn't need a degree in psychology to read the expression in the tense set of Donovan's jaw, the cold light in his hazel eyes. He greeted his employer first, then looked back at Julia, forcing an obligatory smile.

Charles Granville jabbed another button, putting his phone call on hold. "What the heck happened to you? No problems at the clubhouse I hope. Not that I want to know—" he greeted Donovan, not pausing long enough for a reply. "This is Dr. Julia Archer. Julia, Storm. I'll be with you in a minute. Just let me finish up this call—" he said, returning to his conversation in Switzerland.

"Pleased to meet you, Doctor." Looking anything but pleased, Donovan briefly shook her hand.

"Call me Julia," she replied with an easy smile.

"Sure," he nodded. She expected him to say something more, but he didn't. He was not going to make this easy for her—easy for either of them.

Taking a seat on the armchair across from her, he poured himself a cup of coffee. He drank it black. She might have guessed. He made no excuse or apology for arriving almost an hour late, she noticed. She might have guessed that too.

He certainly didn't possess the generic looks of a team manager. Didn't they all have potbellies and thinning hair? His stomach was flat as a board, his chestnut-brown hair thick, slightly curly, sparked with attractive strands of gray. She guessed his age to be about thirty-seven. Overall, he appeared to be in excellent condition, ready to jog out onto the diamond himself if the circumstances so demanded.

He looked uncomfortable in his gray suit, Julia noticed. He tugged on his collar, as if the red-and-blue-striped tie was strangling him. Was it nerves? Or was he more used to wearing a team uniform, rather than this corporate costume? The conservative, commonplace suit looked quite wonderful on his uncommonly fit body, she thought. Julia was quite used to the sight of an athletic physique. Still, Donovan's rated a second, secret glance.

He was sipping his coffee, the bone-china cup looking small and fragile in his large hand. Then he met her curious blue eyes over the cup's rim. Julia managed a calm smile. Never give ground, don't let the other guy know he's got you rattled, her father had always told her, which seemed an especially valuable bit of advice to recall at that particular moment.

"Charlie seems to think you can help the Eagles," Donovan said, setting his cup down.

"Possibly—it's hard to say for sure at this point—should I infer from that statement that you don't?" she added.

"Doesn't matter what I think. I'm just another hired hand."

"A modest way to describe yourself, Mr. Donovan, from what I've heard," Julia replied diplomatically. Though they both knew it wasn't modesty at all, more like blatant sarcasm.

"Well, I'm a modest guy. I guess you haven't heard everything about me *yet*," he replied. "Ever work with any ball players before?"

So he was laying his cards on the table, no phony small talk to warm her up. Well, better this way, she thought, than waltzing around each other for the next hour.

"No, I haven't. But I don't think that will present a great problem," she answered him in an equally direct manner. "The fundamental principles of performance remain the same, whether a person is swinging a golf club, or a baseball bat...." Julia began to explain.

"It all depends on who's swinging what, if you ask me," Storm cut her off. He sat back in his chair, that same brooding look on his face. Like a large stick of dynamite with a very short fuse. A disturbingly attractive stick of dynamite, Julia thought.

"To a certain extent you're right, of course," she agreed, maintaining a reasonable tone. "But the performance of any physical task can be improved dramatically, not only by physical training, but by the type of coaching I do," Julia explained. "Especially when professional athletes with the ability and training lose their concentration, their mental edge—"

"So in other words, you're saying that baseball is all in a guy's head?" Storm interrupted again. "Sort of like sex?"

"Exactly like sex, Mr. Donovan. Although, that's not quite the example I would have used," Julia said evenly. She could feel herself blushing. Her thirty-one-year-old body should have outgrown that silly physiological response. She had hoped Donovan wouldn't notice. Was he trying to scare her off? If so, he had a surprise coming. She could play hardball too, just like the big boys. "I'm not qualified as a sex therapist, however. Do you think sexual dysfunction is the problem your players are experiencing this season?"

"Hell no! . . . I mean that's *not* what I was trying to say at all," he grumbled.

"Excuse me, I suppose I misunderstood." Julia feigned an innocent look. "What did you mean?"

"Sorry I was so tied up with that call. Now, let's get down to some important business." Charles Granville walked over, then sat down next to Storm, conveniently saving the manager the trouble of explaining himself. For the moment anyway, she thought.

With some prodding from Granville, Storm began explaining to Julia the specific problems with his team. There were absentminded outfielders, power pitchers who had lost their "pop," and home-run hitters who couldn't get to first base with a map and compass.

Julia listened attentively, made notes, and asked questions.

Storm was a fitting nickname, she thought as Donovan spoke. He was imposing all right, far more intense than she had expected. He was also surprisingly articulate. Not the slow-talking, tobacco-chewing, "good ol' boy" type that she had found dominated the baseball scene. The subject matter was close to his heart. But the expressions on his handsome, rough-hewn features didn't give much away. Probably an excellent poker player, too.

"So, what's the prognosis, Doc?" Charles Granville asked playfully once Storm had finished. "Any hope for our patient?"

"There is always plenty of hope, Charlie," Julia assured him with a smile. "I'll have to go over these notes again. But so far, I think I can find partial solutions for, if not completely overcome, most of the performance problems you've cited."

"*Exactly* what I wanted to hear," the older man nodded encouragingly. "You're just the wake-up call that the club needs, Julia.... Didn't I promise you that, Storm?" He turned to Donovan, forcing him to voice some opinion of Julia.

"That she is," Donovan agreed quietly. The way his gaze moved slowly over her face, breasts and legs at that moment made every nerve in Julia's body tingle as she became acutely aware of the effect his slow appraisal was having on her. At the same time, it made her angry. Just another ploy to unsettle her, to get the upper hand. She met his gaze with one of obvious irritation. He didn't seem to notice.

"I want you to be my special guest at the game to-night, Julia," Charlie said. "Best seat in the house in my private box. You can see for yourself what needs to be done."

"I'd like that very much. But I have to get back to San Diego tonight. I'm leaving on an eight o'clock flight."

Although Charlie looked genuinely disappointed, she was sure that Donovan was happy to hear she would be out of his hair so quickly. For now, at least. Again, she could feel the manager looking at her. She forced herself to ignore him.

"I'll have some videos of their recent games sent to your hotel," Charlie promised her.

"Thank you. That will be very helpful."

"If you have any questions—any questions at all, you call me," Charlie insisted. "Or Storm—"

"Excuse me, Charlie," Storm cut in abruptly, as if he couldn't stand hearing another word regarding how helpful he would be to Julia. "I think it's time I got back to the stadium." Without waiting to be excused by his employer, Donovan rose from his seat.

"Just a minute, Storm," Charlie said curtly. "I think we're done here. Why don't you give Julia a lift back to her hotel? It's on your way."

"Of course, I'd be delighted," he said, smoothly.

He would be delighted to chauffeur her off the nearest pier, Julia thought. Still, she had no choice but to leave Granville's office with him.

Julia shook hands with Charlie, agreeing to call him with her decision over the weekend. His lawyers had already drawn up a contract, which he handed to her in a large manila envelope. The Eagles were playing a three-game series in San Diego next week. If she accepted the job, Charlie expected her to begin working with the club immediately. It was all happening very quickly, Julia thought as she and Donovan left Granville's office. But sometimes the best things in life come upon you suddenly, it was better to act without having too much time to think.

"Hey, Storm—who's pitching tonight?" Granville's secretary asked as Julia and the manager passed through the outer office. The pretty blonde gave Storm a look that could have been poured over a waffle, Julia noticed.

"Randy Hunt. He'll have his good stuff working tonight, I think," Storm replied with an optimistic smile. A deep dimple creased one cheek, tiny laugh lines fanning out the corners of his long-lashed, hazel eyes. Damned if he wasn't the most attractive man she had met in a long, long time, Julia thought. She realized it was the first time she'd seen him smile like that, though they had been together nearly two hours.

As Storm continued to answer the flirtatious blonde's questions without paying the least bit of attention to Julia, she felt her patience growing thin. She wondered if she had suddenly become invisible. It was not only rude, but absolutely adolescent behavior. Didn't he think she had better things to do with her time than wait out this 'junior high' flirting session? And besides, he never smiled at *me* like that, Julia thought crossly as she stalked over to the elevator, impatiently jabbing the button.

The elevator arrived, packed with the lunch-hour rush. "I've got to be going, Mr. Donovan," Julia called briskly over her shoulder. She stepped into the car, managing to fit herself into a minuscule space. "Don't worry about dropping me off. I'm sure I'll find a cab."

Donovan turned, catching a glimpse of her as the doors began to close. Before Julia could say, "bases loaded" he had reached the elevator, then adroitly held the doors open just long enough to jump aboard.

"What's your rush, Doctor?" As soon as the doors closed, Julia found herself stuck between a wall of Granville's employees and Donovan's hard body. "I thought your flight wasn't until eight."

He was so close she could have tipped her head slightly to test the inviting roughness of his jaw with her cheek. No trouble at all. The errant thought was unnerving, making the close space seem even stuffier.

"It might have occurred to you that I may have other appointments today," Julia replied tersely. She tilted her head back at a ridiculous angle in order to better her view of his face. But when he looked down at her, their lips were so close, she stared straight ahead again at his chest. "In any case...I didn't want you to cut your conversation short on my account...."

"Betsy just loves to talk baseball," Donovan said, referring to the secretary with yet another annoyingly bright smile. "You should have hung around. You might have learned something."

"I'm sure I would have," Julia replied dryly. Something about major-league eyelash batting, at any rate.

The woman behind Julia coughed, shifting a pile of folders in her arms. Julia was suddenly pushed forward, her body plastered head-to-toe against Dono-

van. She held her breath, trying to ignore the feeling
of her breasts pressed against his muscular chest, the
warmth of his thigh through her thin linen skirt. A
hopeless effort, she realized, when it sometimes took
about three dates before she found herself quite this
intimately entangled with a man. They were not far
from a point where, under slightly different circumstances, Julia would have entertained some serious
thought about birth control.

"Easy does it, Doctor." Storm lightly took hold of
her shoulders as Julia regained her balance. "Are you
trying to test my reflexes?" he asked in a low voice, his
breath tickling her ear.

"Not intentionally. . . ." And the man did not mean
his knee caps, Julia thought. She felt hot color flood
her cheeks. This time he was enjoying every second of
it. "Are you trying to test my patience with your cute
remarks?"

He smiled down at her. Not the smile he had given
Granville's secretary, rather, one that revealed his
recognition of a worthy opponent.

"Your reflexes are pretty darned sharp. No doubt
about it," he replied, ignoring her question. "I could
use you in my infield."

The elevator finally stopped and the doors opened.
The crowd spilled out into the lobby. Julia breathed a
sigh of relief.

"My car's in the lot down the block." Donovan ri-
fled his pockets for his parking stub. "This way." He
held the heavy glass door open for Julia and they
walked out onto the street.

It was as if they had stepped into a steam bath, Julia thought, as she slipped on her sunglasses. Her

stylish linen suit, a wide-shouldered, bright blue blazer with matching blue skirt, were clinging to her like plastic wrap after they had walked only half a block.

"This town could use some rain to cool things down," Julia said, trying to pick a neutral topic of conversation. "I predict thundershowers," she added, looking up at the hazy sky.

"Hope not. Hard to play baseball in the rain," Donovan replied without looking at her. "The guys just can't seem to hold on to the umbrellas when they have the bats and gloves in their hands."

"Yes, that must be a problem," Julia replied in an equally serious tone. "All right, I'll reschedule the showers for late tonight, after the ninth inning. How does that sound?"

"Much obliged. Charlie never mentioned rainmaking was yet another one of your talents, Dr. Archer," he added in the same nettling, ironic tone. "Although he did say you've been known to work miracles."

"I was going to walk across the river to my hotel, just to keep in shape," Julia replied, casting him a sidelong glance. "It's kind of you to offer me a ride."

"That's me—honest, kind and helpful," Storm muttered. When they had reached the parking lot, Storm gave his ticket to the attendant. He unfastened the top buttons of his shirt and loosened his tie. Then, he slipped off his suit jacket. Finally, with a casually deft motion, slung it over his shoulder.

"A regular Boy Scout," Julia replied dryly, knowing that was the last image Donovan brought to mind, his dark mat of chest hair showing at the top of his opened shirt.

She glanced away, wishing she could open some buttons and take off her suit jacket too. But she didn't dare. She was sure her white silk blouse now made her look as if she were a contestant in a wet T-shirt contest. Julia decided she would rather melt into a puddle on Donovan's car upholstery than be ogled all the way to the hotel.

"I made it all the way to Eagle. Remind me to show you my merit badges sometime."

"I'm sure I'd be very impressed," she replied, trying her best not to sound as sarcastic as he did. "While we're on the subject of Eagles," she added in a friendlier tone, "why don't you help me out, Storm? Tell me why you object so strongly to my working with the team. Is it because I'm a woman?" she asked him bluntly. "Or rather because you don't think I know enough about baseball? Or you don't believe this kind of coaching works?"

"How about *all* of the above?" Donovan cut in.

"Maybe if you let me explain my methodology, my techniques...."

"Spare me the science lesson about right brain *this*, left brain *that*," Storm shot back. "Charlie already filled me in on all the hocus-pocus."

It took a lot of provocation to make Julia angry. But Donovan was rapidly wearing her good nature ragged. Pushing her sunglasses up on her head, she turned to face him.

"You are being very unreasonable, Mr. Donovan. And very shortsighted, I might add. The kind of work I do is the future for professional sports. I have documented proof that my 'hocus-pocus' works," Julia said, managing somehow to keep from yelling at him right there in the middle of the parking lot. "I think you might ask yourself why you're so resistant to accepting help."

"Since you've got me on the couch, Doctor, at least you can get the diagnosis right," Storm replied with a dark scowl on his handsome face. "I'll tell you what I'm *resistant* to—I'm *resistant* to idly watching someone like you con Charlie Granville out of a bundle."

"Take advantage of Granville!..." Julia was so shocked by the accusation that she was practically speechless. "Are you out of your mind?"

"Figures—before I was 'resistant,' now that I really hit the nail on the head, you say I'm stark raving mad," he dryly observed. "Okay, fine. You're the expert. But even a lunatic like me can see that Charlie is flat-out desperate to help the team. He'll pay any amount to anyone who tells him what he wants to hear. Even some flaky, west coast shrink who doesn't know a shortstop from a bus stop." Julia tried interrupting him, to no avail. "However, she knows exactly what to say and how to say it—don't you?"

Julia had a few choice words for him all right. She was anxious to call Donovan names that were rarely heard outside the locker room. Nevertheless, she held her tongue, silently counting to ten.

She refused to argue another minute with this man. If he could not discuss his objections in a reasonable manner, she wasn't going to listen to any more of his insults.

"To the contrary, Mr. Donovan," she replied taking a deep breath. "I have no idea what to *say* to you at this point. It appears that we are unable to discuss this situation reasonably. You have twisted my every word into either a joke, or an insult." Julia slipped her sunglasses down over her eyes again. Clutching her leather briefcase under one arm, she angrily stalked out of the parking lot. "I think our conversation is finished. I'd prefer taking a cab after all."

Donovan looked startled, even followed her for a few steps, looking as if he might apologize for a moment. But his expression soon turned into a stony mask.

"Suit yourself, Dr. Archer...." He shouted after her as he watched her victoriously hail a cab. "Have a nice trip back to San Diego."

"I will!" Julia called back to him. She got into the cab and slammed the door. "The Ritz Carlton, please," she told the driver.

Her heart was pounding double time as the cab pulled into the midday traffic. She didn't dare glance back at Donovan. She was angry at him, moreover, she was disappointed with herself for losing control of the situation—and her own temper. That wasn't like her. She had hoped that talking to him without Charlie present would clear the air. But somehow, the talk had turned into a public shouting match.

Julia turned her face toward the breeze from the open window, while fingering the manila envelope in her lap. She had a lot to consider before taking on the Eagles and their impossible manager. Donovan had an uncanny way of putting her on the defensive. Julia wasn't used to it.

The Eagles getting their feathers plucked in a 10-0 shutout was not a pretty sight, Julia thought as she watched and sipped her diet soda. Although she'd turned down Granville's invitation to watch the game from his comfortable private box, her flight out of Boston was delayed, so Julia ended up watching all nine pitiful innings from a bar stool in an airport lounge.

Somewhere about the fifth inning and about the fifth error in the Eagle outfield, Julia had stopped taking notes. After every goofy play, the coverage showed Donovan in the dugout. Baseball managers were generally known for their stoic, unreadable expressions. Donovan's face, however, showed every reaction. Reading his lips wasn't difficult either, Julia could comprehend every unbroadcastable expletive. More than once, he leaped onto the field to argue a call with an umpire so forcefully he was nearly thrown out of the game.

For some inexplicable reason, watching Donovan watch his team get beaten to a pulp by a team that was far inferior to the Eagles made Julia so edgy she munched down an entire bowl of nut mix. Naturally she blamed Donovan when her stomach began to ache. After, she felt annoyed about all the needless calories, as if the man hadn't already caused her enough aggravation for one day.

In their closing comments, the network sportscasters sounded more as if they were delivering a eulogy than a postgame wrap-up. As the defeated Eagles left their dugout with bowed heads, once again Donovan's face appeared on the bar's big-screen TV. Julia's own audio system had shut down. No longer hearing the commentary, her entire attention focused on Donovan's larger-than-life image. She forgot about the nut mix, even their angry parting in the parking lot. His disappointed, frustrated expression touched some tender place inside her.

There only remained a pure, compelling impulse to help him. She suddenly realized that she would take Granville's offer. That was what she wanted to do. She would help Donovan, even if he insisted on fighting her for a while.

Then Julia shook her head, surprised at her impulsive thoughts. It simply wasn't like her to make snap decisions about such important situations. She had to read through the contracts, look over her notes from the meeting, consider the pros and cons. Sleep on it a day or two. That was her process for reaching major decisions. Not by staring at some stranger's sad, but determined expression on a TV screen. Donovan's passion about his ball club was admirable, but basically irrelevant to her decision, she reminded herself.

# Two

---

All weekend long, Julia's thoughts were consumed with the question of whether or not she should accept the job with the Eagles. On Sunday afternoon, she decided to sort out her indecision in the most logical, orderly way she knew. After a relaxing walk on the beach, she sat down on her towel, then diagramed a prospectus with a plus column on one side, a minus column on the other.

At the top of the positive column she wrote, "Excellent chance for research on team morale theories." Julia had been looking for a chance to test out her ideas on team psychology. She was eager to verify her findings, and have the results published, before someone else in her field beat her to the punch.

Working with the Eagles would provide an ideal situation for her research. It was an uncanny stroke of luck to have a major-league ball team tossed in her lap, all of whom could be conveniently used as "guinea pigs." Julia bit down on the tip of her pencil. Was she dumb enough to pass up this opportunity?

On the next two lines she wrote, "Embarrassingly huge salary. Ridiculously generous bonuses contingent on whether the Eagles win the pennant and World Series." Granville's lawyers had skillfully plumped up the contract with some rather tempting bait. That was for sure. When the list was finished, to her surprise the plus side reached at least halfway down the page.

In the minus column however, Julia had written just two words. "Storm Donovan." She stared at the list for a few moments, wondering how the accumulative pros could suddenly look so paltry next to one big *con*. Shaking her head, Julia put the pad aside. There it was in black and white. Julia could no longer impede the truth.

This . . . *thing* about Donovan really is ridiculous! Am I going to let some threatened, insecure "jock" intimidate me into passing up the biggest chance of my career, she asked herself. No way!

The beach was almost empty. Julia hugged her knees to her chest, as she watched an orange sun slip slowly behind the cresting waves. She guessed it was just about six o'clock on the East Coast. The Eagles had most likely finished their afternoon game in Boston, she thought—another loss probably. Now, they were packing up for their road trip to the West.

This was a perfect moment to call Charlie Granville, Julia thought as she stood up, brushing some sand off her bottom. She'd go home right away, then tell him she was accepting his job offer. Tonight, she'd make Charles Granville a very happy man. As for Storm Donovan . . . She could imagine his reaction.

As Julia had predicted, Charles Granville was delighted to hear her answer. "Don't worry about Storm," he told her just before hanging up. "He'll come around."

Julia ended the conversation feeling she had made the right choice. Charlie was right. Donovan, like any other pouting little boy, would get over it. He might make her life miserable for a while. But once he sees that his team is back on the scoreboard, Julia assured herself, his attitude toward me will change.

The inevitable phone call from Donovan came early the next morning. In the middle of her first cup of coffee, Julia picked up the receiver to hear the team manager's unmistakable voice on the other end of the line. She braced herself, anticipating the worst.

"Julia? It's Storm. . . . Did I wake you?"

"No, not at all. I've been up for a while." She had been up and out running on the beach already, more out of nervous energy than habit. But he didn't have to know that. "I guess you heard from Charlie last night that I'm . . ."

"Yeah, we spoke," he cut in abruptly. "We're scheduled for an afternoon game today, so I've got to get moving. How about dinner tonight? I think we should talk."

"Uh—sure. That sounds like a good idea." It sounded like something Charlie had suggested—rather, ordered—as a way of clearing the air, Julia thought. She only hoped their meal together wouldn't deteriorate into a food fight.

Although Julia offered to meet Storm at the restaurant of his choice, he insisted on picking her up. She gave him directions to her house, then said goodbye.

Clearly he wasn't a man to waste any time with small talk, she thought with a wry smile. But he hadn't sounded half as upset over the news as she'd expected. Maybe he'd come around to accepting the situation, Julia thought hopefully. Maybe dinner won't be so awful after all.

Julia spent the rest of the day in her office, making phone calls, tying up loose ends so that her schedule for the next few weeks would be completely clear for the Eagles.

When she got home at six, she knew it was time to face the big question: what to wear for her dinner date with Storm? Her closet was packed with clothes, although nothing seemed appropriate for their meeting. "It's too late to run down to the store for the latest cut in a suit of armor...." Julia mumbled to herself as she sifted through her choices.

She pulled out her standard "little black dinner dress," then shoved it back again. Black was too suggestive. A tan linen suit? No, tan was too "blah." Pink was too cute. Yellow? She didn't want to look like Miss Have a Nice Day. She always looked good in blue but blue was so predictable. Polka dots? Too frivolous. Stripes? Too sedate.

Of course, there was always red. Julia held a lipstick-red dress next to herself, as she appraised her reflection in the mirror. It was a dress that never failed to elicit a certain reaction from men. Recalling that reaction, she quickly jammed it back into her closet. Red was just too...red.

Some time later, after showering and drying her hair, she decided on white. Symbolic of a white flag, signifying the call for a truce. The perfect color for starting off with a clean slate. There were buttons trailing up the front of her linen dress and a waist-cinching belt. Its tailored lines were offset by a low square neckline with straps that crossed in back.

"You'll do," Julia thought assessing her image in the bedroom mirror. Even though the formfitting bodice, which bared her shoulders, didn't look very businesslike. She clipped on ivory-and-gold earrings, then lifted her hair for a sparing spray of her favorite perfume. Why was she getting so nervous about this dinner anyway? It wasn't a real "date."

The doorbell rang, Julia took a deep, calming breath. Was it eight o'clock already? At least he was punctual. As she left the bedroom, Julia reached into her closet once more for a white linen blazer. She tossed it over her shoulders, while grabbing her purse. She wanted to signal a truce. Not unconditional surrender.

"Right on time," Julia greeted Storm as she opened the door. He smiled, then walked inside. He was wearing a navy-blue sport jacket, a light blue shirt and white pants. She had forgotten how good-looking he was. Maybe she should have suggested lunch instead of dinner.

"Were the directions okay?" she asked him.

"Just fine. This is a nice neighborhood. You didn't mention that you lived so close to the beach."

"No...I guess I didn't." And when was I supposed to mention that, Julia wondered. While we were exchanging snide remarks in Charlie's office? Or when we were yelling at each other in the parking lot? But she forced a pleasant smile. He was trying to be friendly, to start over again on the proper footing. She would certainly hold up her end.

"The beach is only about a block away, right down the hill. You can see the ocean from the kitchen window....Well, if you stand on a chair..." she added, feeling a little silly for mentioning it at all.

"And if the neighbors have trimmed their hedges?" Storm finished for her with a smile.

"Something like that," Julia laughed. A lethal dimple creased his cheek. She caught his gaze for an instant, then looked away.

"Nice place," he said, glancing into the living room, which was located off the foyer. "I like the way you've furnished it." He took a few steps into the room to take a closer look at a large abstract painting that was hanging over the sofa. Julia would not have guessed that Donovan's taste veered toward the modern, spare look of her decor. Something more traditional— American primitive seemed more in keeping with his character, she thought. Was he just trying to get on her good side?

He squinted at the painting, the look on his face more or less confirming her suspicions. "Nice," he said simply.

"Do you like abstract impressionism?" she asked him, mischievously.

"Uh—yeah, sure..." Storm said, turning to smile at her. "Old baseball cards are more my speed though. I have quite an impressive collection at home."

"Well, you know what they say, 'Beauty is in the eye of the beholder.'"

"Very true," Storm nodded, the corner of his mouth lifted in the hint of a smile. The look he gave her then made her feel suddenly self-conscious and very aware of being alone with him in her apartment.

"I'll just get my keys before we go," she said.

"Sure," he said smoothly. She could feel him watching her walk back into the foyer. She felt better putting even that small distance between them.

She could have politely offered him a drink before they left. Instead, she was eager to get him out of her house for some reason. He was hard to deal with when he was argumentative, Julia thought. However, he was definitely dangerous now that he was pouring on the charm.

When she returned, keys in hand, he was barely a step behind her. He reached to open the door for her, his nearness again sounding distant alarms. For Julia, it promised to be a long evening.

The Mexican restaurant Storm had chosen was not far from Julia's apartment. Like so many places in the area, it had an airy, casually elegant atmosphere, and expensive prices. The hostess offered them a table outside, on a terrace bordered by arches of fragrant, trellised roses. They were white roses, too, her favorite. She remarked on it to Storm as they walked to the table. When they were seated, Julia noticed that the patio overlooked the beach, which lay beneath a flight of stone steps. As the sun was setting, the sky above the ocean looked beautiful.

As if reading her mind, Storm said, "There's a work of art for you. One I can appreciate anyway."

Julia smiled at him, while picking up her menu. "Too bad we can't collect sunsets like baseball cards.

We could take out our favorite ones to look at any-time we wished.''

"Maybe it's a good thing we can't," Storm said after a moment. "They wouldn't be as special then, or as precious. We value them more because they're not ours to keep, sealed away in an old shoe box.''

"Perhaps," Julia said, looking back at what was left of the sunset. The conversation had taken a rather serious turn, she thought. Storm's reflective, sensitive side surprised her. At this rate, they'd be discussing existential philosophy before the waiter arrived to take their order.

She wanted to ask him about the game the Eagles had played that afternoon with the San Diego Padres. The Eagles had lost again, by a score of 6-2. She wondered if the team was a subject better left until later. Instead, she asked Storm about the flight from Boston. Then they talked a bit about the weather in Boston, the smog in L.A., the traffic on the freeways and other inconsequential subjects that they couldn't possibly disagree over.

The waiter soon returned with a bottle of white wine Storm had ordered, then with a flourish he served them each a glass. There was a pause in their conversation. But not an uncomfortable silence, Julia noticed. Somewhere between the sunset and the traffic report, she had begun to feel quite relaxed with him.

"I want to apologize for the way I behaved the last time we met," Storm said then. "Some of the things I said were...well, totally out of line." He stared down at his plate a moment, looking momentarily embarrassed. "Especially out in the parking lot. I'm lucky you didn't take a swing at me with your briefcase.''

She smiled, then took a sip of her wine. The last thing she had expected was an apology. She had to add bravery to the list of his other attributes.

"The thought did cross my mind. Luckily I managed to control myself."

"So I noticed. You seem like a woman who has plenty of that…self-control, I mean." Storm glanced at her over the rim of his wineglass, the candlelight flickering over the strong lines of his face.

He was more than handsome, she thought. When their eyes met, Julia noticed his look of amusement.

"You make it sound like an affliction," she said with a laugh. "Restraint can come in rather handy. You should try it sometime."

He had the good grace to appear somewhat mollified then. "I honestly admire people who can control their temper," he assured her. "It's just that I've never quite gotten the hang of it myself."

"I can coach you on it, if you like," Julia suggested. "When I have some spare time from working with the team."

It was the first reference either of them had made to Julia working with the Eagles. Naturally, Julia thought it was the perfect segue to a subject she was eager to discuss.

"You can put me at the bottom of your list," he replied. "I think my temper is the only thing keeping that team awake lately." He sighed as he shook his head. But, beyond that, he didn't seem interested in talking about the team or Julia's new job quite yet.

"I have to admit, I'm curious about you, Julia," he said, turning the conversation back to her. "Your desire to become a psychologist is one thing. But how did you come to settle on sport psyche? Why not do whatever shrinks normally do?''

''You mean, 'Why would a nice girl like you want to hang around locker rooms, instead of setting yourself up in a cozy little office listening to people's problems all day?'''

''Something like that.'' He smiled at her. The flash in his eyes made her heart skip a beat.

''My office does have a couch,'' she assured him.

''Maybe I can drop by and tell you a few of my dreams, Doctor...if you're interested.''

''Dream analysis isn't exactly my specialty,'' Julia replied lightly, although inside, she felt anything but casual.

''But it might be fun all the same, don't you think?'' he persisted.

''I guess that depends on what you dream about, Storm.'' Julia was trying her darndest not to let him see how his warm looks and provocative little jokes were unsettling her. She wasn't sure that she was doing a very good job of it however. The self-control Storm had made such a point about earlier seemed to be failing her tonight. Maybe it was the wine. Or the way Storm was looking at her.

''But to get back to your question,'' she said, trying to control her runaway imagination. ''My interest in athletics began way before I got interested in psychology. I grew up with three older brothers, who I tried extremely hard to keep up with. I was a bit of a tomboy.''

''You were a tomboy, huh?'' Storm's gaze swept over her with a warm look. ''Doesn't show anyplace now.''

"I have a few battle scars on my knees to prove it,"
she said, trying her best to ignore the way he was ap-
praising her. "My brothers could dare me into doing
just about anything. And the Archer home team was
equipped for every season—baseball, tennis, foot-
ball, hockey. All we needed was a basketball hoop in
the dining room. My mother used to tell guests that the
decor was 'early gymnasium,'" Julia added, making
Storm laugh. "My dad was an instructor and coach at
UCLA, so he didn't mind at all."

She hadn't meant to tell him about her father. It had
just slipped out.

"Your father coached at UCLA?" Before she could
answer he said, "Your father is Dan Archer?" Julia
just nodded. He seemed impressed, as most people in
her profession were when they learned that she was
related to the famous tennis coach. She only hoped he
wouldn't start thinking nepotism had been the key to
her success.

"I bet you have a wicked serve."

"I'm a fairly good player," she said modestly. "I
used to play a lot more when I was in high school and
college. My father really wanted me to compete
professionally. I did, for a short time when I was a
teenager." She couldn't understand why she was suddenly telling Storm so much about herself. It wasn't
like her to spill her life story over a glass of wine and
a Mexican dinner.

"What happened? Pressure get to you?"

"I thrived on the competition," Julia said with a
small laugh. "It felt just like home.... You forgot
about those three older brothers."

"Yes—I suppose I did," Storm said, laughing then too.

"I loved tennis. And I was good at the game. But when I was a sophomore in college I discovered something that fascinated me even more than my daydreams of playing center court at the U.S. Open."

"Psychology?" Storm said.

Julia nodded. "I lost my killer serve, but I think it was worth it. After a while, I realized I was more interested in studying how professional athletes could excel than in being one myself."

"Very interesting." Storm leaned back in his chair, regarding her with a thoughtful look.

She wished she was more of a psychic than a psychologist then. Was he thinking less of her for dropping out of the pro-tennis circuit, assuming she just couldn't cut it professionally? His opinion of her shouldn't have mattered but she didn't want him thinking she was a defeatist.

"It must have been tough for you to make that choice," Storm said finally. "I imagine you worried about disappointing your father."

"Yes—I did," Julia answered honestly. His insight surprised her. "He took it pretty hard. He really thought I was making a mistake. But I had to do what I felt was right for me. You can't live out someone else's dreams."

"No, you can't," Storm agreed, swirling the wine left at the bottom of his glass. "Most days, it's hard enough living out your own."

"Well, I've answered your questions, Storm," Julia said, trying to steer the conversation in a lighter direction. "Now I have one for you. Ready?"

"Nothing embarrassing I hope?"

"I don't believe so. It's just something I've wondered about you."

"Oh?" He looked interested, even flattered to hear he had been in her thoughts. "What was that, Julia? How I got to be such an argumentative, son-of-a—Irishman?"

He made her laugh then. "That too," she admitted, holding his gaze for a long moment. A tingling wave of heat swept through her. She tried to get her thoughts back on track. "Actually I was wondering about your name."

"My name?"

"Yes—I mean, is it really Storm? Or is that a nickname?"

"You want to know what my real name is? That's what you've been wondering about me?"

"Among other things . . . yes." She nodded, giving him a puzzled look. "Is there some reason you don't want to tell me?"

"Uh—no." He ran his hand through his hair, then looked down at his plate. "It's just that I took a lot of teasing about it when I was a kid."

She hadn't meant to hit a sore spot with her question. His obvious discomfort was so uncharacteristic. Somehow glimpsing this moment of weakness made Julia like him even more.

"Oh—well, you don't have to tell me if you don't want to. . . ."

"No—no, I'll tell you. My real name is Francis," he admitted. "Francis Michael—the Michael for my grandfather."

"And the Francis?" Julia prodded him.

"The family story goes something like this—the night I was born a hurricane hit the Boston area. My father couldn't get my mother to a hospital so I was born at home. A neighbor, who was a nurse, came over to help with the delivery and my father told her, boy or girl, if the baby lived he swore he'd name it after her...."

"Francis?" Julia asked.

"It could have been worse, I suppose," he said finally. "Her name could have been Amelia, or Lucy—"

"It's a nice name," Julia said, laughing with him. "I've always liked the name Francis. It's very musical."

"It's very *pretty* is what you mean. In the neighborhood where I grew up, it was tough enough staying out of trouble without walking around with a name like Francis."

Julia had to laugh at the look on his face. "You got into a few fistfights defending your 'girly' name, I guess?"

"My nose didn't always slant to the left like this." He pointed to a bump in the bridge of his nose. Julia hadn't noticed it before. She thought he had a perfectly fine nose. One that went well with his perfectly wonderful face.

"So you lost your 'girly' name and started calling yourself Storm to scare off the school-yard bullies?"

"My dad's idea. He had to keep his promise. But he did want me to survive to high-school graduation. Not as a prizefighter either."

"As a baseball player?"

"You got it. He sure loved the game. He was a cop and worked nights a lot. In the spring, he would let me play hooky from school. We'd sneak off to the afternoon games at Fenway. It was a little secret we kept from my mother," Storm confessed, his voice dropping down to a conspiratorial whisper.

"He must be very proud of you, managing the Eagles."

"Well, I think hc would have been. He died almost fifteen years ago. Right after my first year in the majors. I got an athletic scholarship to Georgia Tech. I wasn't much of a student," he admitted. "But I stuck it out, then signed with the St. Louis Cardinals my senior year. He saw me win twenty games that season and take the Cy Young Award," Storm said, mentioning a very important award given each year to the league's outstanding pitcher.

Julia was quite impressed. She had assumed Storm had played baseball himself for a while before becoming a manager. Although she'd had no idea he'd had such a distinguished career.

"What happened... Why did you stop pitching?" As soon as Julia voiced the question she wondered if she should have. Perhaps she was getting too personal now.

"Line drive smashed my elbow. The kind of surgical techniques they patch a guy up with these days hadn't been developed yet. Even if I'd been fortunate enough to receive today's treatment, there was no guarantee that I could have pitched again."

Julia felt a bit stunned by his answer. She couldn't imagine what that must have been like for him, having such a brilliant future wiped out by a freak accident.

"I'm so sorry—" she said finally. "That must have been an awful moment, finding out you couldn't play anymore."

"That it was," he admitted. "But I was young. I knew I couldn't just give up. I couldn't let a bad break beat me altogether. That wasn't how I was brought up. I made it to the majors and had one great season. That's more than most ex-jocks pushing forty can say," he added with a wry smile.

"Good for you," Julia said, smiling back at him. She admired his attitude. Everyone experiences setbacks, but certain people never move on. Storm certainly hadn't allowed the unfortunate end of his career as a player to make him bitter. "I'm surprised that you didn't leave baseball," she said then.

"I did. I spent about two years in the *real* world but I was like a fish out of water away from a ball club. I had to come back. I took a job as pitching coach for the Eagles' minor league club down in Florida."

"And the rest is history," Julia said. She already knew from Charles Granville that Storm was one of the youngest managers to come along in many years, also one of the most winning managers the Eagles had ever seen.

"Well, it could be history if the Eagles win the pennant and the World Series. But the history books don't care much about wishes that *almost* come true."

"No, they don't, do they?" she replied. "So that's your dream now, seeing the Eagles in the World Series?"

"Are we back to dreams again, Doc?" he asked without answering her question. "I thought you said it wasn't your beat."

"I did, didn't I?" The waiter had cleared away their dinner and served them both coffee. Julia took a sip of hers.

He obviously didn't want to talk more about his aspirations, so she didn't press him. She was actually amazed that they had gotten this far. And so painlessly. The evening was giving her a new respect for Storm. He was so different from the men she usually spent time with.

Although she and Storm didn't always agree, or even speak the same language at times, she found it refreshing to meet a man with such strong convictions, such a passion for his work. Once again, just as in the moment in the airport bar, she felt that impulse to help him realize his dream for the Eagles. She had a feeling that together, they could do it. Together with Storm, she might be able to do just about anything.

When she glanced over at him, he was watching her. His warm look was almost as powerful as a touch.

"What are you looking so serious about?" he asked in a quiet, teasing tone.

For a moment Julia considered being honest with him. Then she caught herself. "I always look serious when I'm considering dessert."

They had played true confessions enough for one night, she thought. They hadn't even talked about her job with the team yet.

"Do you want something?" he laughed, glancing around for the waiter. "I just love to watch a woman who really enjoys dessert. It's so rare."

"Well, here I am, one of a dying breed," Julia admitted with a grin. "I consider chocolate one of the three basic food groups."

"Is that so? I've heard that eating chocolate is a substitute for being in love." He sat back gazing at her, his arms crossed over his broad chest. "Something to do with brain chemistry...well, you would know more about it than I would, Doc. Is that true?"

"Not that I'm aware of." She looked away, then cleared her throat. She had in fact read an article about the phenomenon only the other day, but she didn't want to admit it. She was saved from any more talk about the subject by the waiter's timely appearance beside the table.

"I think I've changed my mind. I'm going to skip dessert tonight, thanks," she said to the waiter.

Smiling at her, Storm asked for the check. Since the only reason they had met for dinner was their business relationship—or lack of one—Julia didn't feel right letting him pay the whole bill.

"May I split that with you?" she asked as he looked over the check.

As he began to reach for his wallet, he said, "What's the matter? The idea of a man buying you dinner too old-fashioned for you?"

"It's not that...." Julia felt flustered, though she didn't know why she should be. "This was more or less a business meeting. There's no reason why you should get stuck with the entire bill." Julia knew she was being perfectly sensible, but the look on Donovan's face seemed to say otherwise. His know-it-all grin would have been annoying, she thought, if it wasn't so damn contagious.

"You like to do things by the book, don't you, Doctor?" he asked with a laugh.

"Maybe...." Despite herself, she smiled back at him. "But no more than you like to take control, Mr. Donovan."

"Wow—" He shook his head, his eyes sparkling in the candlelight. "You have a mean pickoff move, ma'am." He was comparing her comeback with a pitcher's quick throw to catch a runner stealing a base.

"You made it too tempting for me, taking such a big lead off the bag," she said, laughing at him.

"Just for that, you have to let me pay," he insisted, placing some bills on the table. "If it makes you feel any better, I'll put it on my expense account, okay?"

"Okay," she said. He'd probably planned to do that all along. But he couldn't resist provoking her, could he?

When were they going to discuss business? She was glad they had gotten to know each other better, hopefully smoothing over the strained feelings from their first meeting. But she wondered why he hadn't said a word yet about the team. It was time one of them broached the subject, she decided.

"I saw some footage of today's game on the news," she said, taking the plunge. "I had a few ideas about working with the pitcher—"

"How about a walk on the beach?" he said, surprising her. Had he been listening to her at all, she wondered.

"All right," Julia said, rising from her chair. He wanted to talk while they walked on the beach. No harm in that, was there?

As they headed for the stone steps that led down to the water, Julia felt his light touch at the small of her back. She knew then, that walking on a moonlit beach with a man like Storm Donovan would never be a completely harmless proposition.

# Three

————

At some point during dinner, Julia had taken off her blazer. It was much cooler down by the water which was what prompted her to slip it over her shoulders again. She soon felt Storm's hands helping her with it. Through the thin material she could feel the warmth of his touch on her shoulders and arms.

"Your jacket is kind of thin. Let me give you mine," he said.

"This will be fine." She tilted her head back to look up at him.

It was very dark and they were suddenly very much alone. She could barely see him, yet felt totally aware of every inch of him standing so close to her. The energy that arced between them was unmistakable. Overwhelming almost.

He lifted her hair up out of her collar, his hands lingering at their task for a moment. His fingertips brushed the cool silky skin on her neck. Julia forgot to breathe for a second. A lick of heat, like brushfire, swept through her from head to toe. She was tempted to close her eyes and step toward him, so tempted to feel his strong arms move up and around her, pulling her close. Instead, she backed away, thankful for the darkness that at least partially hid her reaction.

"Uh—why don't we walk a bit?" she suggested.

She moved away from him a step or two, then slipped off her shoes. What was happening to her? Get hold of yourself, Julia, an inner voice admonished. Before you do something you'll be sorry for.

"I want to speak to you about the team, Storm," she added, in a firmer voice. "I've sketched a plan for working with the players who need the most help first—"

"Must you?" He cut in. His tone told Julia he had anything but baseball on his mind.

Trying to ignore him, she picked up her pace. "Oh, so you trust me to do whatever I think best?"

"Wait a second. That's not exactly what I mean, Julia." Matching her steps, he came up quickly beside her.

She liked the way he said her name. It did things to her that she tried to ignore. Pulling her jacket closer around her, she kept walking.

"Well, I don't know what you meant *exactly*," she said, even though she had a pretty good guess, "but it seems to me you've been trying to avoid talking about the club all night. Is there any reason for that?"

"Is there any reason you can't go 'off duty' for more than five minutes at a stretch?"

"What?" She stopped walking, then turned to face him.

"You heard me." He was staring at her, but it was hard to read the expression on his face. He didn't look angry, Julia thought. The tone of his voice sounded more like exasperation. "Didn't you enjoy our dinner conversation? I did."

"I—yes, of course I did. It's just that—" It was hard to gather her thoughts with him staring at her like that, standing so close to her, the wind off the water swirling his dark hair. There was an urge to touch him, to reach up and smooth his hair back off his forehead. She couldn't even remember anymore what they were arguing about. Men never did this to her! What was it about this one?

"Just that what?" he asked softly, taking a dangerous step forward.

"Just that—" As she took a step back, she could feel the water move up around her ankles, her bare feet sinking into the wet sand. Just the way her common sense was all but swamped by her attraction to this man. "I'm pleased you've come around to accepting the idea of me working with the team. What I don't understand is why you're so reluctant to get down to business."

He was quiet for a moment. "Who said I've come around to accepting anything? Did Charlie tell you that?"

"No—but I thought from the way you've been acting that—"

"Listen," he cut in, "I haven't *accepted* anything. I still don't like the idea one *bit*."

"Perhaps accepting is too strong a word. Tolerating the situation then . . ."

"I'm still hoping to talk you out of it."

"What?" Julia stared at him, wide-eyed.

"You heard me."

"Is that why you suggested the moonlit stroll?" she asked, feeling her temper rise. She felt so ridiculous. So foolish! The way she'd let her fantasies run wild.

"Uh—no. That part wasn't planned." He coughed, then, looking slightly embarrassed, stuck his hands in his pockets. "Actually I was hoping to make my pitch while we were still having dinner. After the wine was opened, but well before the food arrived."

"Really?" Julia asked coolly. So nothing had changed at all. This entire evening of getting-to-know-you charm was a carefully orchestrated setup. Of all people, she should have seen through it. Instead, she let her attraction to him get in the way. She turned, looking out at the ocean, hugging her arms around herself for warmth. "What happened? You and the waiter get your signals crossed?"

"Guess I got . . . distracted."

"Distracted?" Julia shook her head in disbelief. "Could it possibly be that maybe, just maybe, getting to know me a little changed your mind? Made you wonder if having me work with the team was such an awful idea after all?"

"Being near you makes me wonder about a lot of things, Julia. I guess that was the distracting part," Storm confessed with a small laugh. "But that doesn't change the way I feel about you, or anybody like you

working with the team. I still think it's a rotten, mis-
guided, ill-advised, desperate idea. And I want you to
know right now that I'm not going to lift one finger to
help you. If you arrive at the stadium tomorrow,
you'd better know what to expect."

"How dare you!" Julia spun around to face him,
sorely tempted to push him right into the water.

"How dare I be honest with you? I thought that's
what folks in your profession arc always aiming for—
getting it out on the table."

"It's hardly your honesty I object to. How dare you
try to intimidate me, bully me, or even wine and dine
me into backing out of this deal. I've been hired to do
a job. That is what I intend to do, with or without your
cooperation, Donovan."

"It will have to be without. We'll see how long
you'll last."

"Really? Well, since we're being so up-front and
honest with each other tonight, I *honestly* think that
you're more interested in shielding your delicate little
ego than seeing the Eagles go to the World Series. In
fact, you're acting more like the lead ape in a baboon
troupe, than a manager whose first concern is to see
his team win."

"Now wait a second, this has nothing to do with my
ego or acting like a lead . . . what did you call me?"

"Baboon. A lower primate with certain socialized
behaviors," she clarified for him. "If you weren't so
concerned about protecting your turf, Donovan,
you'd at least give me a chance." His expression
hardened at that remark, but he didn't challenge her.
"The baboon's courting behavior however is a bit
more sincere," Julia added, wondering now if she was

going too far. "Unlike humans, they don't know how to be so...manipulative."

"Manipulative? When was I doing *that*?"

"When *weren't* you is more to the point! The restaurant, the wine, the walk on the beach—" Reviewing the evening made it abundantly clear how easily she had been drawn into his scheme. "The perfect seduction scene...when your real purposes were anything but—"

"Julia, slow down a second. You've got it all wrong—" He made a move to touch her, but she pulled away.

"I have nothing left to say to you. Good night!" She turned, running up the beach. She only wanted to get as far away from him, as fast as possible. She heard him call her name, but hoped he wouldn't follow.

He did follow her though and it took only moments for him to catch up to her. Julia knew it was senseless to keep running. They were both short of breath, unable to speak. She could feel the tears welling up and was angry at herself for having such a powerful reaction to him. Taking hold of her shoulders, Storm turned her around to face him. Unable to will herself to move away, she stared at him, warning him off with her eyes.

"Julia—" he began. "Damn it, what's the sense..." he sighed. Wrapping his arms around her, he drew her to him. Julia knew she should push him away; instead, she felt herself falling against him, urging him closer, the hard lines of his body merging magically, mysteriously with her own slender, giving form.

When his mouth came down against hers, she heard him breathe her name on a deep, soulful sigh. She trembled inside as he tightened his grasp, their tongues swirling together in a deliciously intimate duel. He teased her, tasted her; beneath the compelling pressure of his kiss, Julia felt herself drifting back, until she was lying on the hard-packed sand, enfolded in Storm's powerful embrace.

"Do you think this is all an act?" he whispered, framing her face in his big hands. "Well...do you?"

Before she could speak his mouth came down on hers again, harder, more insistent. With deep, devouring kisses he continued their argument where his words had left off. Julia answered him, kiss for kiss, touch for touch, her hands moving hungrily over his hard shoulders and powerful back. She savored the feel of his body crushed intimately against hers; the weight of him pressing her down into the sand felt so satisfying, so right.

She forgot he was the *enemy*, determined to block her at every turn. She had forgotten how, only moments ago, she'd been angry at him. His strong hands moved over her, his warm lips kissing her face, her hair, caressing the curve of her throat, exploring the soft swell of skin just above her breasts.

Julia could lie to Storm. But she couldn't lie to herself. From the very first minute they'd met, she had secretly longed to know what kissing and touching him would be like. The reality of it was more passionate, more intense than any fantasy. Their coming together was like a jagged burst of lightning, white hot. Julia had never known anything quite like it. The pressure of his mouth on hers became more ardent, more demanding, beckoning Julia to surrender totally to his sensuous assault. She didn't stop to think of all the reasons she shouldn't have let this happen, but allowed herself to savor every sensation the touch of Storm's hands and lips inspired.

"For an expert on human behavior, Doctor," he whispered huskily between quick, hard kisses, "you've certainly misread my signals."

Julia allowed herself the pleasure of one last kiss, then twisted her face to the side, her eyes opened. Suddenly the spell was broken. Yes, she had misunderstood his motives tonight during dinner.

What was she doing, rolling around in the sand with him like some...lovesick teenager! She tried to move away, but Storm resisted her, his heavy body holding her in place. He stared down at her, wearing a puzzled expression on his face.

"Julia?...What's the matter?"

"Let me up now...please," she said softly, avoiding his eyes. She slid out of his arms, then sat up. She took a deep breath as she pushed her hair back from her face. "This is getting a little...out of control."

"More than a little for some of us—" He propped his head up on his hand, looking bewildered. "Care to argue with that?"

"Storm—you know what I mean. You proved your point. Let's just leave it at that, all right?"

"For pity's sake, woman—" He sat up, appearing to be in a state Julia would have termed aggressive bewilderment. "You make it sound like I was conducting a laboratory experiment!"

If his feelings weren't honestly hurt, he was doing a good job of making her think so. She felt a twinge of remorse for sounding so cold and clinical. But she didn't know any other way to handle the situation. At least one that wouldn't lead back into trouble.

"You were trying to prove that there's an...an attraction between us," she said carefully. "You could have asked me. I wouldn't have denied it." She stood up, brushing the sand off her clothes.

"Well that's some comfort." He came to his feet, narrowing the distance between them. He seemed bigger, more menacing. "A cold one maybe, but some—"

"Good. Then we understand each other," Julia cut in. "We can forget this ever happened, okay? I don't want to get involved with you, Storm. Not that way. I hope we can get along as colleagues, perhaps even as friends. But this attraction we have is only going to make things more complicated." She took a deep, calming breath. As long as she didn't look into his eyes, she could keep her thoughts clear. "Besides," she added, "it's really rather...irrelevant. Don't you think?"

"Irrelevant?" His laugh was a harsh sound. He looked down at her, his arms crossed over his chest. "I'm sorry to be such an illogical, overly emotional guy, Julia. But I can't turn my feelings on and off like a water faucet. I don't think our attraction—or whatever you want to call it—is irrelevant. And I don't want to pretend it doesn't exist."

"While we're working together you'll have to," she insisted, holding her ground. Why did he have to make this difficult for her? Couldn't he just accept a simple "thanks, but no thanks" so they could go about their business?

"What if I won't? What if I can't?"

"Then you're stuck with a case of unrequited lust. Too bad. I hear it's the most painful kind." She started walking toward the stairs again and he followed her.

"Very funny."

"I'm serious."

"So am *I*. And I think you are one damn remarkable woman," he said, sounding almost angry to have come to that conclusion. "But I don't want you working with my ball club!"

"Get used to it, Donovan. I'm not going away."

They had finally reached the stairs. Julia spun around and looked at him. She was somewhat out of breath and totally out of patience. "I'll see you tomorrow morning at the stadium," she called over her shoulder as she ran up the stairs. "Nine o'clock would be good. We have a lot to talk about."

"Wait a second—I'm driving you home. Did you forget?"

"No you're not. I'm taking a cab. Again." The look she gave him from the top of the stairs stopped him in his tracks. "And try a cold shower tonight for your *condition*. It really works."

# Four

When Storm arrived at the stadium the next afternoon, the talk was of nothing else but the 'strange babe' who'd been hanging around the clubhouse since eight o'clock that morning. He wondered what Julia had done all that time. Watch the locker-room attendants bring in fresh towels?

"Hello, Julia. Sleep well?"

"What there was of it." She had actually had a rotten night's sleep, all because of him. Now seated behind the desk in the office for the visiting team manager, her papers and folders were spread out all over the place. She took her time before she looked up at him. "Why didn't you tell me nobody gets here until late afternoon?"

"You didn't ask." Storm shrugged, then took off his red baseball jacket. Unfortunately he looked as good in his jeans and a gray, Eagles T-shirt as he had in his sport jacket the night before. Better, Julia thought. "We have a night game today, didn't you check the schedule?"

Julia knew the schedule. But for some ridiculous reason, she had assumed that when she told Storm she would meet him at the stadium at nine, and he didn't contradict her, they had made an appointment. Next time she'd know better.

"No harm done," she said lightly. "I had a chance to look around." Enough time to try out every seat in the stadium, but she didn't say that to Storm. "...And do some work with these computer printouts I found on your desk."

She wondered if he was going to be mad at her for looking through the papers on his desk. When she'd found a stack of computer printouts that showed each player's batting average in every game over the past month, she couldn't resist. Especially since no one was around to tell her not to.

"So glad you found something interesting to read while you waited. Is there any chance of me taking a look at them now?" he asked in a tone laced with sarcasm.

"Of course. Don't be silly." She picked them up to hand them over, then realized she was sitting at his desk. Not simply sitting, she had taken it over. A man with his territorial instincts could not be pleased about that. "I was just getting out of your way." She stood up, quickly gathering her things.

"But not far enough, I'm afraid," Storm replied dryly. "Not say—back to your apartment?"

Pushing by him with her pile of papers and folders, Julia didn't even spare him a glance. "Where can I put this stuff?"

"In your car?"

"Storm—" Julia began in a warning tone.

There was a sharp knock on the door, which sounded to Julia just then like the bell at the end of round one.

"Come in," Storm called out. The man who entered glanced briefly at Julia, but didn't bat an eye. As if an argumentative woman in Donovan's office was a common sight, she thought.

"What's up, Eddie?"

"Nothing good, pal," Eddie answered in a serious tone. He was dark and wiry, a certain type Julia had known all her life. She didn't know what he did, but would have bet anything that he was a trainer or coach. "Randy Hunt ain't going to be able to pitch tonight. Kid hurt his hand. His pinkie on his pitching hand."

"How the hell did he do that?" Donovan roared. He threw down the stack of computer readouts, creating a blizzard of papers as they flew all over the office. Julia braced herself, but Eddie didn't flinch a muscle. He seemed quite conditioned to Donovan's explosive temper.

"Jammed it last night playing Donkey Kong in the hotel bar," Eddie explained calmly.

"Donkey Kong? What the hell is Donkey Kong?"

"You know—one of them video games."

"A video game?" Storm was yelling even louder now. "We're going to get swept in this series because that dumb kid had to stay up all night pumping quarters into a . . . *Donkey Kong*?''

"Luckily it ain't broken. The kid's finger I mean," Eddie said, not bothering to answer Storm's question. "But he won't be in no shape to pitch for at least a week. He can't get nothing on his fastball."

"Great! That's dandy. My best southpaw benched by a damn Donkey Kong," Storm moaned. He shook his head. "Go tell Osgood he's starting tonight."

"Sure thing," Eddie said. "But you know the kid's a little high-strung. He's not going to be so thrilled going out there on three days rest. . . ."

"Who cares if he's *thrilled*? As long as he gets the damn ball over the plate," Storm replied in a dull roar. "Besides, he's the only left-hander available. If he gets roughed up, we'll go to the bull pen early." Julia knew enough about the game to understand that Storm was referring to the relief pitchers, who usually came into the game in the final innings, after the starting pitcher had tired. "Go over the lineup with him. I'll be out in a minute."

Sweeping some papers aside, he located the phone, then proceeded to punch in a number. Feeling dismissed, Julia followed Eddie out the door, closing it behind her.

"Is he always like that before a game?" Julia asked Eddie.

"Like what?"

"So . . . easily upset?"

"He's got good reason to be upset about Hunt riding the bench." Eddie laughed. "Besides, that was nothing. You got to see him when he's really ticked. I once seen Storm kick a watercooler so hard he broke his toe.''

''Broke his toe?'' Julia repeated in disbelief.

''That's right. You should have seen the watercooler,'' Eddie added. ''Managed to keep it out of the papers though....'' Then Eddie's friendly expression suddenly changed. ''What are you, a reporter or something?''

As his eyes skimmed over her, Julia realized he was looking for a press pass.

''No, I'm not a reporter,'' she assured him, glad to see him relax again. ''I'm going to be working with the team. Today's my first day. Charlie Granville hired me to do some—'' She hesitated to tell Eddie that her work was psychological in nature. The term was so easily misunderstood ''—a special type of coaching.''

''Oh, yeah—you must be the shrink Charlie was sending down,'' Eddie said knowingly.

''Who told you that?''

''Word gets around,'' he shrugged. ''Well, you got your work cut out for you, Doc. Plenty of screws loose in this clubhouse.''

''I'm not that kind of psychologist—'' Julia began to explain.

''Yeah? Well, maybe you ought to be,'' Eddie replied with a crooked grin. ''Eddie Carlucci, the pitching coach,'' he added, extending his hand for her to shake.

''Julia Archer,'' she replied, glad to be making a friend. ''Nice to meet you.''

''Same here,'' he said shortly. ''Good luck. I got to find Osgood,'' he said, peering around the locker room. ''Kid's got some homework to do in a hurry.''

"Oh, sure—" Julia nodded. Players had begun to drift into the locker room, which explained the steady rise in the noise level. Some of them had started to change into their uniforms. They hardly seemed to notice her, standing by the office door. But she suddenly felt quite awkward. Although, from past experience, she surmised that more than a few of these guys weren't the least bit bashful about showing off their bodies.

The office door flew open and as Storm made his hasty exit, he nearly knocked her over. "Sorry—" he said. Then he realized it was Julia. "Enjoying the show?"

"I was just coming back to ask you where I should go to watch the game," she said, hoping he wouldn't use the inquiry as a chance to make another wisecrack. "How about the dugout?"

"What? And have the media breathing down my neck, asking a million questions about who you are, what you're doing in my dugout? No way, lady."

It was more or less the answer she had expected. His wariness about the media, however, gave her a good idea.

"Maybe I should watch from the press box. I'm sure I could sneak my way in without a pass. I'd probably learn a lot up there, don't you think?"

Storm's eyes narrowed. He knew what she was doing. He also knew he'd been outmaneuvered. "I can give you a pass for some nice box seats on the third-base line. You won't miss a trick."

"Thanks. That sounds perfect," Julia replied, trying not to gloat over her small, but significant victory.

He mumbled something unintelligible in reply. She followed him back into the office. He began to rummage through the papers on the ravaged desk top.

"I know you're busy right now. But I was wondering, when do you plan to introduce me to the team?"

The look he gave her then seemed to say that he had never planned for such a moment to take place. In fact, he had hoped with all his heart her association with the Eagles would never have gotten even this far. He handed her the box-seat pass and rubbed the back of his neck.

"Won't you meet them by just hanging around?"

"Oh, you mean as in hanging around the locker room while they get dressed? Or outside tonight with the autograph hounds? Or maybe I can stop by the hotel bar after the game. At the risk of being mistaken for a baseball groupie."

"They're going to take you for a groupie anyway," he said flatly. "Ever think of that?"

"I'm sure I can handle it," she replied in a flip tone.

"Famous last words," he said, more to himself than her. The flash of fire in his eyes told her he was remembering last night and their passionate embrace on the beach. Julia remembered, too. In fact, every time she looked at him it was hard to think of anything else. She held his gaze for a split second, then looked away.

"...On second thought, I think it's my players I'd better worry about," he said.

"Would you just answer my original question, Donovan?" Julia struggled to sound calm, as if she were in control of her emotions.

"Sorry...." He shrugged, then hurriedly glanced at his watch. "I've got to get out of here. You can find your way to the seats, I'm sure. We'll figure this out later. Don't eat too many hot dogs.''

''I hate hot dogs.'' She waited until he had his hand on the doorknob. ''And don't worry—I'll find some way to introduce myself....'' She let her voice trail off suggestively. She didn't really know what she would do, but she hoped her tone would give Storm second thoughts about trying to brush her off.

She held her breath. He turned the knob, but didn't open the door. Finally, barely glancing over his shoulder to look at her, he said, ''Come back down here after the game. I'll give you an official introduction, okay?''

She would have preferred an introduction before the game, but before she could argue the point, he was out the door, making his way out to the field.

Instead of going meekly up to her box seat to watch the workout, Julia decided to push her luck a bit further. Outside the locker room she wandered down a long dark corridor called the tunnel, which led to the players' entrance to the field. She loved the look of a baseball diamond. The grass was such a brilliant green it was absolute perfection.

Some of the players were taking batting practice. Others were warming up by soft-tossing the ball or hitting ground balls to each other. Don was on the sidelines talking to another coach. On his handsome face he had that same brooding look that Julia was getting to know much too well for her own peace of mind. Once he had changed out of his street clothes, Julia found herself identifying strongly with that old adage about most women having a weakness for men in uniform.

Hoping to avoid him, she walked down the first-base line toward the visiting team's bull pen where the pitching staff were being put through their paces. Two pitchers were throwing to catchers crouched at the far end of the pen. A group of secondary pitchers stood around watching, talking to one another in between chewing wads of gum or chewing tobacco.

Julia, noticing Osgood, walked over to talk to him. He had the largest lump of something in his mouth; it looked almost the size of a baseball under his cheek. He was tall, lanky, with pale blond hair showing at the edges of his baseball cap. Large, frightened-looking blue eyes peered at her from under the brim.

"Hi, I'm Julia Archer," she said, introducing herself. He looked at her warily, rearranging the lump in his mouth to the other cheek.

"You allowed to be over here? They're not supposed to let anybody on the field—" He looked around nervously.

"I'm working with the team," she explained. "Today is my first day. Storm didn't get a chance to introduce me earlier."

"Oh—okay." The pitcher stared at her, chewing his gum. He looked so young. Barely twenty-one, she guessed. "My name is Julia. You're Wally Osgood, right?"

"Yeah—that's me," he nodded, but didn't offer any more information. Julia could see she had her work cut out for her, still, she persisted.

"I understand from Eddie that you're pitching tonight."

"Umm—yeah. I wasn't supposed to, but Randy Hunt banged up his hand—" His words trailed off. It seemed as if he wanted to talk to her, though he wasn't sure of how much he was allowed to say.

"—playing video games," she finished for him. "Donkey Kong, wasn't it?"

"That's right." He laughed, looking as if he were relieved to let his guard down.

"How do you feel?" Julia asked him.

"Okay, I guess." He shrugged, chewing his gum with more conviction. Every muscle of his body language suggested to Julia's trained eye that he didn't feel "okay" at all. He felt as tight as a bowstring and very apprehensive. "Eddie says my curveball has some good stuff on it tonight."

"Ever pitch against this team before?"

"Once or twice this season. I didn't do so good," he admitted. "I only stayed in the game about four innings last time I faced them. Sure hope I do better tonight," he confided.

"I hope you do too," Julia said sincerely. "I think I can teach you something that will help your pitching, too. At least, help you go out on the mound feeling more relaxed."

"Help me?" He gave a nervous laugh, then looked down at his glove. "How could you do that? I never heard of a woman pitching coach. But there's a woman umpire in the minors, so I guess anything is possible."

"No, I'm not a pitching coach. I'm a sport performance psychologist, Wally. Do you know what that is?"

"Sure, I heard about that stuff," he nodded. "I read an article about it the other day in a magazine."

Julia wasn't sure if he really knew what her work was about, but an article in a magazine was a start.

"I was hired to help the team get out of their slump," she explained. "I'd like to teach the players how to use certain techniques to work through blocks, which would enable them to operate at their peak level of performance."

"Get back in the groove you mean?"

"Exactly. But first, it's important to be relaxed out there, to feel confident, to have a good attitude." Athletes choke when they lose a relaxed—or loose mind-set. Their bodies can only be as relaxed and free-flowing as their state of mind.

"You got that right." He nodded his head, this time chewing his gum more thoughtfully in agreement. "I am feeling a little nervous tonight," he admitted.

"Would you like to learn a special way to relax? It will only take a few minutes?"

"You don't want to hypnotize me or anything like that, do you?"

"Nothing like that." Julia laughed.

"I'll try anything once I guess. Can we do it out-side?"

"Sure—" she glanced around, and saw two folding chairs at a vacant corner of the workout area. "Let's sit down back there, where it's quiet."

A few minutes later, Julia led Wally through a brief relaxation exercise. First he took deep breaths. The technique completely relaxed each muscle group in his body. Then, with Julia's voice guiding him, he visualized himself doing something he really enjoyed. Wally told her he loved to go trout fishing. He described the cool mountain lakes where he'd gone fishing with his father and brothers since he was a boy. He returned, annually, during the off-season. Julia told him to picture everything about that setting, the sights, sounds and smells. She told him to imagine casting his line, waiting for a bite, fighting it in on the line, reeling in the biggest trout he'd ever caught.

When he opened his eyes again, he gave her a broad smile. He had color in his cheeks, she noticed. Wally didn't look nearly as drawn or tense as he had. Waiting until he was ready to speak, she continued to observe him.

"Gee—I feel good," he said finally. He stood up, then punched his fist into his glove. "I mean *real* good.... Know what I mean?"

"This exercise is brief, but it gets good results' she said. "If you start to feel tense again later, remember that it's important to take deep breaths. With you shoulders back, inhale through your nose, exhale through your mouth. Will you remember that?"

"Sure thing," he nodded. "Deep breaths," he re peated, as if it was a magic code word.

"*Osgood*, what are you doing back here?" Storm's sharp words shattered the calm mood. He had come up on them so suddenly neither Julia nor Wally had noticed him. "Why aren't you going over the lineup with Eddie?"

"I was uh—just talking to Julia. About my breathing..."

"Your breathing? What about it?" Storm demanded, sounding alarmed.

Julia could see that Wally was confused. She had given him the impression that it was perfectly all right for them to talk. But his manager was sending the opposite message. The pitcher's newly found tranquillity was blown to smithereens by Storm's interrogation.

"She said I shouldn't forget out on the mound to, uh—to uh, you know..." he motioned with his glove, "...keep breathing."

"Brilliant advice." Storm's gaze narrowed. He tossed Osgood a baseball and the pitcher caught it with a reflex snap of his glove. "Go toss some sinkers. I'll be over in a minute."

"Sure, Storm." Glancing briefly at Julia, Wally walked away.

Storm turned to Julia, looking like an enraged mother bear, she thought. She faced him calmly. "I think you could have handled that conversation differently," she said. "You didn't have to intimidate him."

"When I want your opinion on how to talk to my pitching staff, I'll ask for it. What the hell were you doing back there?"

"The job I was hired for."

"What did you say to him?" he persisted in a harsher tone. "I have a right to know."

"You heard him." Julia shrugged. "I told him to keep breathing," she said innocently. "Does that advice contradict any of your training theories?"

His gaze locked with hers. Julia could feel her heart pounding furiously, but she willed herself not to show him that he'd rattled her. These nasty confrontations would be a heck of a lot easier if I wasn't so damn attracted to him, she thought then. Why did she have to feel like that? Even now. Even when he showed her time and again that he was a stubborn, thick-headed, son-of-a . . .

"You are making me crazy," he said in a soft, menacing voice. He came closer, staring directly into her eyes.

"Maybe you should see somebody about that." She couldn't resist venturing a small smile.

He was about to reply, when Eddie called from the far end of the bull pen where Wally Osgood had started to warm up.

"Hey, Storm—" Eddie called. "Come over here. I want you to see something."

"Be right there," he called back. He turned to Julia, "We'll finish this conversation later. And I want some straight answers."

"Really?" She wouldn't mind explaining any of her methodology to him. In fact, she really wanted him to understand. But she hated that belligerent note in his voice. She wasn't one of his rookie pitchers. He couldn't push her around. "Don't hold your breath, Donovan," she advised.

He had already turned his back to her and was walking away. But by the twitch in his shoulder blade, Julia knew he had heard her.

Although the Eagles lost the ball game by a score of 4-2, Wally Osgood pitched until the seventh inning. In his past few starts, Storm had been replacing him with a reliever midway through the game. Even though the Padres won, Osgood managed to strike out six, which was much better than his average.

After the game, Julia made her way through the departing crowd, on down to Storm's office. The small bare room was vacant but she saw the manager's duffle bag and jacket on a chair, which meant he'd return sooner or later. A peek in the locker room was all she needed to see that he hadn't called the team together to meet her as he had promised. Feeling slightly defeated, she sat in a chair and waited for him.

Somebody knocked on the door. "Come in," Julia said. It was Eddie. He poked his head through the doorway. "I was waiting to see Storm," Julia said.

"Oh—he's not here, huh?" Eddie started to leave, off in search of Storm again, Julia assumed. Then he abruptly changed his mind and came back in. "Heh, I want to ask you something, Julia. Just between you and me," he added in a more confidential tone as he closed the door, "what did you do to Osgood?"

"I didn't *do* anything to him," Julia said wearily. "We talked for a few minutes, then I taught him a little relaxation technique."

"That must have been some relaxating... *whatever*. Did you see the movement on that kid's hanging slider? It just hung there and broke. Hung there, like a butterfly or something. And broke." Eddie had a rapturous look on his face, as if he'd been describing a work of genius. "They couldn't touch it."

"Isn't that called a dead fish?" Julia asked.

"Like right out of the pitching-school textbook."

"He doesn't usually throw that pitch?"

"Not like *that* he doesn't."

The door flew open. Storm saw Eddie and Julia talking together, and his expression darkened.

"Hey, Storm, I want to talk to you about Osgood—" Eddie began excitedly.

"Later, Eddie." Although he was speaking to the pitching coach, his gaze was fixed on Julia. "The good doctor and I have to discuss something. Privately."

"Sure. Catch you later." Eddie walked out, closing the door. Storm sat on the edge of the desk with his arms crossed over his chest.

"You said you were going to call the team together right after the game to meet me," Julia said.

"I forgot." The expression on his face was an unreadable mask. Julia knew he was lying. But she also knew it was futile to argue with him about it right now. He obviously had his own agenda.

"How do you think Osgood did tonight?" he asked in a deceptively pleasant manner.

"I've never seen him pitch before so it's hard to say...." What was he up to? she wondered. She had the distinct feeling she was being baited. "You didn't take him out of the game until the seventh inning," she said. "So, I'd say he pitched pretty well."

"So would I. So would anyone who knows anything about baseball. But don't start getting any funny ideas that I think you had anything to do with it, okay?"

"Okay," Julia shrugged, allowing herself a secret smile. Judging from the volume and vehemence of his denial, it was clear that Storm was thoroughly convinced her talk with Osgood was the reason for the pitcher's stellar performance. "And certainly not his dead fish," she meekly added just to test his reaction.

"Especially *not* the dead fish," he bellowed back. "We've been working with him on that pitch for months. You come along, talk to the kid for five minutes about heaven only knows what—"

"We talked about his hobbies—fishing mostly," she quietly cut in.

"Fishing, bowling, stamp collecting—who cares? You tell him to take a deep breath and presto, Wally Osgood looks like the next Dwight Gooden!"

"He did look dangerous with that pitch, didn't he?" she murmured.

"Sorry, lady, it doesn't work like that. It was just a coincidence. A fluke. A freak thing," he said waving his arms carelessly in the air.

Storm stood up, then began pacing around the small office in front of Julia's chair. The man had an amazing amount of energy. When he had strong feelings about a subject, there was no holding him back. Her errant thoughts strayed as she wondered what it would be like to be the focus of that whirling tornado of passionate energy. "It was just his night to get it all together out there. His performance had nothing to do with you"

"I never said it did," Julia replied with a slight shrug.

"Don't humor me."

Julia stood up and faced him. "Just answer one question—you're positive my conversation with Osgood had no effect on the way he pitched. Correct?"

"Absolutely."

"Then you can't possibly object if I work with him more tomorrow."

"Are you kidding? He's finally got it together out there. He's finally putting something on the ball. You think for one second I'm going to let you near him again? You'll get him all confused!"

"Like the way he was tonight you mean?"

"That boy isn't any rocket scientist, Julia," he replied, ignoring her point completely. "Once you start putting all kinds of wild ideas in his head, he won't be able to chew gum and zip up his pants at the same time."

From what Julia had seen of Osgood's gum-chewing prowess, she had the feeling the pitcher could 'chaw' his way through a major earthquake, or any other such cataclysmic event, no problem. It was an irrelevant point however.

She felt totally frustrated. But she was far from giving up. "Can't you be reasonable about this? For just a minute?"

"Can't you?" He looked down at her. He was standing very close, his face just inches from her own. Wearing his baseball uniform, his dark hair mussed to perfection, he looked better than any man had a right to, she thought. She tried to look away from his steady gaze, but she couldn't.

"Julia—" The sound of her name in that low tone sent a shiver of heat through her body. He sighed. "Why?"

"Why what?" Her voice could only register a whisper.

"Why do you have to be so obstinate?" She shouldn't have let him put his hands on her hips and draw her to him. But she did. "So beautiful. And sharp. And obstinate."

"Storm—" She could barely speak when she looked up at him. She pressed her hands to his hard chest, not quite sure if she wanted to pull away, or get closer. "I know what you're trying to do. You're not getting rid of me that easily."

"Good. Don't move a muscle...." He bent to kiss her. Julia couldn't resist feeling for an instant the wonderful pressure of his mouth on hers. Of all the men who'd ever crossed her path, why did *this* one have to be capable of having such a powerful effect on her? They kissed. Then kissed again, longer, harder, her mouth easily coaxed open by the gentle probing of his tongue.

Finally she turned away, but didn't quite move out of his arms. With her head nestled against his shoulder she sighed. "I'm sorry I let this happen again...."

"That makes one of us," he laughed, brushing a kiss against her hair. "Ever since I walked in here this afternoon, I've found it difficult to keep my hands off you."

She felt the same way about him. But that didn't mean she had to fall into his arms when he so much as glanced her way.

"I thought we settled this last night," Julia said, withdrawing from him. "We can't get involved that way. I just won't."

"Ah, yes.... It's coming back to me now." He watched Julia as she gathered up her jacket and briefcase. She moved to the door, barely sparing him a glance. "Guess the cold shower didn't work."

"Take another one," she suggested. The face he made at her in reply was mostly comical.

"The bus for the airport leaves the hotel tomorrow at nine." For the first time all evening his voice sounded tired, resigned. But Julia knew better than to think she'd won.

"I know," she replied. The public relations assistant who traveled with the team had kept her apprised of the travel arrangements and schedules.

"Be there on time. We won't wait for you," he warned her.

"I didn't think you would." Without saying goodnight she let herself out of the office, thinking that a cold shower was what she needed as well.

# Five

Okay, listen up, you guys. We have a new staff member here I want you to meet, Dr. Julia Archer." Storm paused, glancing at Julia. She could see that he was practically choking on every word. In another minute, she'd be forced to throw her arms around him and administer the Heimlich maneuver. "Some of you may have met her already. She's a sport performance psychologist and she will be travelling with us, uh—offering her expertise," he concluded diplomatically.

*Offering,* he had said. Not that he was encouraging anybody to listen, she thought.

All eyes turned to Julia. The club had traveled to Los Angeles to play the Dodgers. Realizing that he could no longer forestall the inevitable, and probably wary of Julia taking matters into her hands, Storm had gathered the team together before batting practice to introduce her.

She stepped out in front of them. Thirty pairs of curious male eyes fixed on her. She was wearing a roomy Eagles T-shirt, jeans and sneakers. Her hair was pulled back in a clip and she wore the minimum dash of makeup. Wanting to draw the least amount of attention to her looks, she hadn't exactly dressed to win any beauty contest. But the way they were looking her over, Julia thought, she might as well have worn a bikini.

"I'm Dr. Archer. Please call me Julia," she began. "I'm glad to be meeting all of you *finally*," she added, with a pointed glance at Storm.

"Some of you may not be familiar with the field of sport performance psychology. But, just as in the more traditional type of coaching, the object is to help you maximize your performance—"

A fidgety group under any circumstances, they looked even more restless than usual. She could see that the idea of a female coach made them nervous. Julia forced a warm, bright smile. But the only truly friendly face in the group was that of Wally Osgood.

"As you all know, playing at your peak has a lot to do with mental fitness, or attitude," she continued. "And of course, the ability to reach a certain level of concentration. Each task that you perform on the field is in part a function of your left brain, and also of your right brain...."

They stared at her blankly, most of them chewing away on something. A guy in the first row took a long, noisy, tobacco-juice-spitting break. Storm caught her eye just then, his face wearing a smug smile. Had she lost them completely? She took a deep breath and plowed on.

"Listen, this team is in a slump. Charlie Granville hired me to get you out of it. You still have a chance to finish at the top of your division. To go to the play-offs and the Series. I'm here because I have faith you can do it."

She had finally gotten their attention. A few almost looked eager to hear more. "I want to set up a private meeting with each of you, to explain more. You may not understand what I do, or how to incorporate my techniques. But they do work. All I ask is that you give them a fair try. Any questions?"

They were quiet. It was hard to tell what they were thinking. From her experience with Osgood the night before, she sensed that perhaps a few were privately thinking that at this point they had nothing to lose. Of course, nobody wanted to be the first one to admit that out loud.

Finally, toward the back of the group she spotted a raised hand. It was Firecracker MacDougal, the team's big home-run hitter who had lately lost his *caboom*.

"Yes?" Julia said eagerly.

"Heck, I'll try some, honey. Where do I sign up?" The other men hooted with laughter.

"Yeah—I'm sold, Doctor," someone else called out. "Where's your office? You single?"

Julia felt the color rising in her cheeks. She managed a small *good sport* smile, but willed herself not to show any other reaction.

Before the wisecracks could get any wilder, Eddie stepped out of the crowd to rescue her. "Okay, you guys. The floor show's over. Let's get to work."

Chatting among themselves, the team gathering broke up. They picked up their equipment and began to head off toward different areas of the field to work out. Julia had thought at least one or two of them would approach her privately. A few flashed her a flirtatious smile as they strolled past, but that seemed to be the extent of their interest in her.

"You look cute in your workout togs, Doc," Storm said with a wink as he walked by. His grin was annoyingly bright. Had she made that poor an impression? "Where did you find that T-shirt? I didn't know it came in circus-tent size."

"I *like* them roomy." She pulled on her sunglasses and crossed her arms over her chest. "Don't they need you out there to direct traffic or something?"

"They know the drill.... Nice day for a ball game, wouldn't you say?" He tipped his head back, taking in the brilliant blue sky.

"There's too much wind blowing toward right field. And you know it. Don't be so nice to me, Donovan. It makes me nervous."

"Why shouldn't I be nice to you?" he asked innocently. "The thing is, I've had a change of heart about this situation, Julia."

"Since yesterday in San Diego? When you all but forbade me to speak to your players because they'd get so confused they'd forget how to zip up their pants?"

"Did I say that?" He grinned, pushing his cap back on his head. "Yeah—I guess I did." He nodded agreeably. "You have an amazing memory. Really."

"Did I do *that* badly up here? I mean, so badly that you're willing to just give me enough rope and watch me—"

"Don't even say it," he cut in solicitously. He flashed another heart-stopping grin, his gaze sliding down over her for one last, quick, sizzling inventory. "Sure wish you'd toss that T-shirt in the dryer next time it goes through the wash," he suggested in a friendly tone as he walked away. "See you later."

Julia stood alone in foul territory, speechless. He was patronizing her! The nerve of that man. Especially since he could have made the problem of gaining the team's trust so much easier for her.

All she had was a team roster and a fairly good idea of which players needed her help the most. She decided that she would handle the situation as a naturalist working out in the wilderness with wild animals might. For a day or two, she would hang around their "natural habitat," merely observe, getting the wild, farouche creatures comfortable with her presence. Ultimately, as she did with Osgood, she could approach them privately, then work to gain their confidence.

Despite his avowed change of heart, she had no doubt Storm would still go out of his way to foul her up. But he couldn't be everywhere at once. She had already made inroads with Eddie Carlucci and Wally Osgood. Perhaps they were already saying good things about her to the others, she thought optimistically.

During the team's series in Los Angeles, Julia stuck to her "Marlin Perkins" imitation. The Eagles lost two of three games to the Dodgers. It was frustrating for her to be on the sidelines with her hands tied. Storm had given her enough rope for that. She tried to be patient, but it was difficult with every loss now critical to the team's standing.

Although she'd never heard Storm say anything openly critical about her, it was obvious to everyone that she'd been thrust at him by Granville. When she dared to approach him while he was talking to the team coaches or a group of players, she felt an arctic blast that would have given the most thick-skinned soul frostbite.

True to his word, Storm had finally stopped trying to chase her away with his histrionics, but he still wanted her to leave his team alone. His latest ploy, however, was obviously to freeze her out. She couldn't do her job if the players and coaches wouldn't deal with her. For the most part, they seemed to take their cues from their manager and he was simply pretending she didn't exist.

The team's next stop was San Francisco for three games with the Giants. The Eagles morale was low. It was shaping up to be the worst road trip of the season. Most of the players were muttering about their eagerness to get back East.

Julia, however, was not looking forward to returning to Boston. At that point, she'd have been with the team about a week and she'd be obliged to tell Granville just how ineffectual she'd been so far. Of course, there was Wally Osgood's amazing new "dead fish" pitch. But she'd never wrangle an ounce of credit away from Donovan for that one. She couldn't go crying to Granville about the manager's adolescent antics however. Granville had warned her right from the start. Storm knew that no matter what he did to undermine her, Granville would never fire him over it. She was the expendable one, that was for sure.

She hated to think that Francis "Thunderclap" Donovan was going to get his way. But in only four days, she already felt her confidence had been considerably worn down. The job would have been hard enough without facing up to his resistance and battling down her attraction to him.

And there were other reasons that the job was harder than she had imagined. The traveling schedule was tough. Baseball must have been invented by nomadic tribes she decided, long before Abner Doubleday ever got the bright idea.

Julia thought she knew a lot about the sport, but she was rapidly finding out that what she didn't know could fill volumes. Hanging around the players these past few days, she felt like a stranger in a strange land. They seemed to be speaking in their own private language and she was lost without subtitles. They had special names for everything, pitches, hits, defensive plays.

Pitchers wanted to throw some *K's*, some smoke, some heat, or the *high* heat. The kind that would remind a guy of Louisiana and the blew-by-you. The worst place to put a ball was right in a guy's wheelhouse where he could do some damage. They worked on their heavy sinker, a wicked Lord Charles, or an off-speed slider, low and away. Then there was a knuckleball, a split-fingered fastball, or even a screwball. There was the pitch they said Rembrandt threw, which just painted the outside corner of the plate. Or the one that came high and inside, so they could sneak into a guy's kitchen and rattle his pots and pans.

Sluggers talked about bloopers, choppers, squibbers, ropes, dunkers, dingers and grounders with eyes.

About getting his foot stuck in the bucket, or letting some pitcher punch his ticket out. A hitter wanted to send a ball down main street and say goodbye Mr. Spaulding. But sometimes a guy had to *sacrifice*. Or even finding a hole would do. In one way or another they all subscribed to Eubie Wheeler's legendary advice to just "hit 'em where they ain't."

Julia tried to listen and absorb all she could, sometimes even taking notes. In only a few days, she became considerably more fluent in *baseball-ese*. But she hesitated to try out some of the more obscure jargon, for fear of using it incorrectly and embarrassing herself.

However, whether she said the words aloud or not, the picturesque phrases soon began seeping into her thoughts. She had to laugh at herself when she realized she'd begun thinking in baseball terminology, particularly during her frequent run-in's with Storm.

In their verbal skirmishes, she would try a hit-and-run play, or put the shift on him in her own mental outfield. More than once, she'd try to make inroads with the team behind his back—or steal second. But Storm didn't miss a move and would either pick her right off the bag for an easy out, or put the tag on her in a rundown.

His former pitching prowess was even more evident, however, when their unavoidable, undeniable male-female chemistry came into the picture. When he ignored her, or feigned a deceptively courteous attitude, she called it his change-up or off-speed pitch, designed to put her purposely off balance. Most often he'd follow it up by sending her some heat, the kind of suggestive looks and remarks that nearly blew her

away. She had to admit that she was having a hard
time staving him off. He hadn't tried to kiss her again
since that night in San Diego, after Osgood's game.
But Julia knew it was only a matter of time before
Donovan would try to put the squeeze play on her.

The Eagles miraculously won two of their three
games with the Giants. Wally Osgood was one of the
winning pitchers. After his game he privately confessed to Julia that he'd been employing her relaxation device on the mound. Whenever things got tough,
he'd transport himself for a moment back to his favorite lake in Arkansas.

Julia was pleased that the technique was working so
well for him. Unfortunately the help she'd given Wally
wasn't common knowledge. Being naturally shy and
a rookie who had just come up to the majors, he
hadn't felt comfortable confiding to any of the other
players that during the most crucial points in the
game, he was taking imaginary fishing trips. Julia was
sure that Eddie Carlucci knew what was going on with
Osgood. But the coach was loyal to Storm. Julia knew
he'd never encourage his pitching staff to work with
her as long as Storm so obviously disapproved of her
*interference*.

So far, Julia had been treated as a virtual social
pariah by the players and coaching staff. The men
were all polite. Some even made it clear that the sight
of a good-looking babe like her on the field every
morning was a mighty fine wake-up call. Still, she was
totally excluded from their off-time social circle, even
when wives or girlfriends of players were present. She
never took it personally, knowing the exclusion was
only due to Storm's powerful influence over them. But

of course, somewhere deep down it still hurt to be snubbed when she asked if she could join a group for breakfast in the hotel. Finding a seat on their bus during the road trips was especially tough.

The problem was easy to ignore, since most of the time the team was either practicing, playing ball, or traveling. In the few, random off-hours, she kept to herself, exercising in the hotel pool or working on her research notes.

The team broke even on their road trip, winning as many games as they had lost. It was respectable baseball, but hardly the stuff that dreams and pennant races are made of. Certainly far below the level of play Julia knew the Eagles were capable of.

After their final game in California, they took a red-eye flight east. When she found her window seat on the plane, she was relieved to see the adjoining seat on the aisle was vacant. She hoped it would stay that way. She didn't feel up to forcing a friendly conversation with any of the less-than-friendly baseball players.

While wearing her cassette player headphones, Julia listened to a tape of her favorite classical pieces. With her eyes closed, she hoped she'd fall asleep before the takeoff.

She was apprehensive about returning to Boston. She was going to call Granville as soon as they landed. Once there she would try to see him before the Eagles played another ball game. It seemed that she had no recourse but to plead her case to the Eagles owner, even if he ended up thinking she was a big crybaby and not professional enough to work around Donovan.

Charlie had seemed a reasonable, even understanding person. Perhaps he would have a talk with Donovan, tell the manager to start cooperating. The worst scenario would be Granville's loss of faith in her abilities, leaving him no alternative but to terminate their contract. Julia bristled inwardly at the thought of leaving the Eagles in such a humiliating way. And *only* because of Storm Donovan's short-sighted, pigheaded . . .

Julia's mental diatribe was cut short by the sensation of someone tugging lightly on her sleeve. Her eyes flew open to find the seat next to her occupied by a dark-haired little girl.

"Want some?" the little girl asked her, holding out a pack of candy. "My mom said your ears won't pop if you suck on one of these."

Julia pulled off her headphones. "Sure—thanks." She took a candy, unwrapped it, then popped it into her mouth. "What's your name?"

"Katie Jo Bradley." Katie leaned past Julia to look out the window. "I like takeoff the best," Katie said, sounding like a very experienced traveler. "Do you?"

"Sometimes—are you on this flight all alone?" Julia asked her. Katie was incredibly wide awake for such a late hour. Julia guessed it was the excitement of traveling. She sure was a talkative little thing.

"Nope—" Katie shook her head. "My mom and little brother are sitting up front. I'm going to walk up to visit them later. Want to come? Gee—you have pretty hair," Katie added. "Can I listen to your tape player?"

Before Julia could reply to any of Katie's questions, the stewardess appeared in the aisle next to them.

"Katie Bradley? We found you a seat up front next to your mom." With a stewardess's typically efficient flair, she scooped up Katie's coloring books and paper dolls, then guided her out into the aisle. "This man was nice enough to switch with you."

The *nice* man finally came into view, sliding by the stewardess to fit his large frame into the economy-class seat. Before Julia could say, "Fasten your seat belt," her new traveling companion was making himself comfortable only inches away.

"Well, what a coincidence," Storm greeted her. "Visiting friends in Boston?"

"None that I know of," she replied, matching his wry tone. "I didn't know you were prone to good deeds, Donovan. Or maybe Katie's brother tried to interview you?"

"The kid couldn't even say 'Dada' yet. Don't get me wrong. I like kids, just fine. But the little guy was teething and this is a six-hour flight."

"Unfortunately...yes."

"You don't have to talk to me, Doc. I won't be insulted," he insisted. "Go ahead, put your earphones back on. Just pretend I'm not here."

Fat chance. Every nerve-ending in her body was flashing an emergency alert signal and he wanted her to act as if he weren't there?

"How about a magazine?" he persisted. Pulling one out of the pocket in front of him, he offered it to her.

"No thanks...I brought a book." She pulled out a thick paperback, ceremoniously opening it, even though she knew she wasn't going to read a word.

The plane had taxied to the runway and began to take off. Storm leafed through the magazine on his lap, although he didn't seem to be interested in reading any of the articles.

"Looking forward to being back in Boston?" she asked him. It was inconvenient to have him sit here, but it was silly to think they could last the entire six-hour flight without speaking to each other.

"I wouldn't mind a good meal at Mario's," he said in a longing tone, "or watching some of that good old, home-field advantage kick in at Fenway."

"What did Charlie say about the road trip?"

"What could he say? Breaking even isn't the worst thing. But it isn't exactly a good thing either. If good things don't start happening for this team pretty soon, we're all in the deep stuff—as in, no joy in Mudville when play-off season rolls around."

Storm's tone was light and offhanded, but Julia knew he was far more concerned than he sounded. She was surprised that he was confiding in her so willingly. But it was very late, they were both very tired. Their defenses were down, and seemed to all but disappear when the cabin lights were dimmed.

"It doesn't have to be like that. There could be joy in Mudville again," she dared to reply in a soft voice, "if you would let me start working with the team."

"Julia—" Leaning his head back on the seat he gave a long sigh. "Are you going to drag me through this conversation again? I'll go sit in the aisle. I swear it. Or maybe in the bathroom. Don't think you've got me cornered here for six hours so that you can—"

"I don't want to talk about it, *either*. Calm down, Storm." She didn't mean to touch his leg with her hand, but she did. Before she could pull it away, he put his larger hand over hers, urging her palm against his hard, warm thigh.

"*That* is not exactly the way to make me feel calmer. It certainly takes my mind off my troubles though...."

"Very funny." Julia pulled her hand away. Her heart was racing. How was she going to last until they reached Boston? At this rate she'd barely make it past Colorado.

"I think it's only fair to warn you. When we get to Boston I plan to talk to Charlie about our problem."

"Which problem is that? The problem I have staying calm around you? I think he'll find that most understandable."

"The fact that you've done all you can so far to keep me away from the players—short of locking me up in an equipment closet."

"Oh, that problem." He nodded in an understanding, almost sympathetic manner. "Well, if you must, you must," he sighed philosophically. "I wonder if you can dial direct to Moscow?"

"Why would I want to?" Julia asked, sitting up straight. Although, the moment she saw the look on Storm's face, she had her answer.

"You said you wanted to complain to Charlie about me, didn't you? He's out of town on a little business trip. Ever hear of *glasnost*?" Storm asked smugly, referring to the new Soviet policy of increased cultural and business relations with the West.

"Golly gee," Julia replied dryly. "I thought it was a new brand of spray-on window cleaner."

"Very funny. I'll have to remember that one," Storm said. "You have a sharp sense of humor, Doc. I like that in a woman," he added generously.

"When will he be back?" Julia asked, ignoring his compliment.

"I don't know." Storm shrugged. "He'll probably stop in Japan on his way back to see the Tokyo Giants play a few games in the league. They sure do love baseball over there."

"So I've heard," Julia said blandly, settling back in her seat. They both knew she wouldn't bother to contact Granville while he was abroad. It looked as if she were back to square one.

"Don't look so upset, honey. Maybe he'll bring you back a little souvenir. You'd look great in a black silk kimono," he teased her, a seductive twinkle in his eyes.

Before she could answer him, a flight attendant came by with an armful of airline bed linen. "Pillow and blanket?" he asked.

"Perfect timing." Storm took enough for both of them. "Now we can really get comfortable. Isn't this cozy?"

"Delightful. I'm going to sleep now," Julia announced. She hit the button on her armrest that made her seat drop back.

"Sweet dreams," Storm said pleasantly.

Trying to ignore him, she slipped the pillow under her head, giving it a solid whack. Spreading out the cover in the cramped space was a bit more awkward, however. Storm had already very quickly arranged his. Afterward he sat there watching her as if the sight of her positioning a blanket over herself was utterly fascinating to him.

"Why don't I get this out of our way?" he suggested, folding up the seat arm in between them. Julia felt unaccountably alarmed watching the only barrier between them disappear into the seat cushions.

"It wasn't bothering me," she said.

"But it might later," he predicted. "When you fall asleep, I mean."

The stage was fully set for a dress rehearsal of "Bedtime with Storm Donovan." From this point on, Julia couldn't fool herself for a minute into thinking that she'd have a wink of sleep until her head hit a pillow in Boston.

"Need some help getting that around you?"

"I can manage, thank—" But before she could say any more, Storm had leaned over and began gently, but not so innocently, tucking the blanket around her. His face very close to hers, he whispered, "Julia, I think we're in trouble."

Julia *knew* they were in trouble. But she wasn't quite sure his idea of trouble matched her own.

"How do you mean?" she managed. She wanted him to kiss her. She couldn't help it. If he didn't kiss her soon, she didn't know what she would do. A long, slow, deep kiss that would last until they reached the Great Lakes.

"I mean," he began, slowly brushing his mouth across hers in a tantalizing motion, "there are no showers on this plane....do you realize that?"

"Showers? What are you talking about?" Her mind was dazed, drugged, slipping into a cloud from the touch of his lips, his solid warmth so close, the tangy intoxicating taste of him....

"I'm talking about my condition, Doc. My unrequited problem? You know, I never asked you—is this contagious?"

"It depends on the other person's resistance," she whispered back, playing along with him.

"Really?" Storm dropped a kiss on her nose, at the corner of her mouth, then one soft kiss on each of her closed eyes. "There's some hope for me? I'm not doomed to spending a good part of my life under cold running water?"

"No hope at all." Julia's hand slipped up around his shoulder, her fingers sliding into his thick dark hair. "I've heard that once you catch it," she whispered breathlessly, "there's absolutely no cure."

She couldn't help herself. She needed to feel the warm pressure of his mouth on hers. If only for a moment. Without stopping to think, she pulled his head down toward her, their lips finally meeting in a deep, hungry kiss.

She sighed at the sheer perfection of it. How could anything that felt this good be so bad for her, she wondered. Beneath the blanket, his hand stole up across her rib cage to softly cup her breast, then liquid fire raced through her veins. Their official altitude was thirty thousand feet, but the bold magic of Storm's touch was quickly sending Julia to the stars.

Her hand slipped under his loose cotton-knit pullover. At that moment, she felt the muscles in his stomach contract. His chest was covered with crisp dark hair. The sensation was so tantalizing, she explored further, eagerly swirling her hand across the hard contours. There was unspoken yearning in her touch, her secret hunger for so much more of him, her secret desire to discover, to enjoy every sexy inch of him.

"Mmm, Julia—" He pulled his mouth away from hers a moment and nuzzled her neck. Taking a deep breath, he pressed her hand, still beneath his shirt, to his heart. She felt its strong, steady throb under her fingers. His skin was feverishly hot. "Feel what you do to me? It's like I just ran a three-minute mile."

"Storm—" she sighed, her cheek pressed to his, "—this is too much. Someone will see us...."

"Everybody's asleep," he whispered back, his lips discovering a silky, ultrasensitive spot on her neck that was definitely one of her danger zones. "Maybe we are too. Maybe I'm dreaming, Julia. Please don't wake me up yet."

He looked into her eyes and a very pure, elemental message passed between them. On some deep, intuitive level, far beyond baseball and their adversarial positions, Julia felt a fateful, undeniable bond with this man. When his mouth moved over hers again in another soul-shattering kiss, her response was undeniably clear. A passionate reply that their dream didn't have to end quite yet.

Soon enough however, she was jarred back to reality by the sound of the captain's voice coming over the address system.

"Looks like we're headin' straight into a high pressure system, folks. And that means some heavy turbulence—"

*Now* he tells me, Julia silently replied as she and Storm slowly parted.

"We've got a bumpy ride ahead, so I suggest y'all return to your seats and fasten up."

The seat-belt sign flashed above them, then the flight attendants began to walk down the aisles, making sure all the passengers were buckling up.

Julia stole a secret glance at Storm as they each searched for their seat belts. "Sounds like we've been rained out," he teased her in a private voice. "Any chance of scheduling a rematch in Boston?"

"I don't think—*Storm!*" While groping around the seat cushions for his belt buckle, his hand had slipped under her bottom. The unexpected contact made her sit bolt upright.

"You're sitting on my seat belt," he said innocently. She quickly lifted up, removing the belt end from under her. "Thank you."

"You're welcome. I'm going to sleep...and I mean it," she said in a no-nonsense tone that made him smile. She pulled down the seat arm between them, then pulled up her blanket to her chin. Closing her eyes, she turned her face to the window.

"Sweet dreams, Julia," Storm whispered in the dark.

Julia pretended not to hear him.

Somehow, bumpy ride and all, Julia eventually managed to fall asleep. When she woke up a few hours later, the arm rest had mysteriously disappeared again. She was snuggled against Storm's solid warmth, her head cushioned on his broad shoulder.

Her eyes opened slowly and soon met his soft gaze. She had the feeling he'd been watching her, waiting patiently for her to wake up. It made her feel cared for, also, somewhat alarmed.

"Have a good rest?" She nodded, knowing she should pull away, but not quite able to. "You were talking in your sleep, Doc," he whispered.

"Oh?" she felt flustered. None of her dreams about Storm were ones she'd care to go public with. She moved away from his seductive warmth, but he still kept his arm draped across her shoulder. "Sorry—you should have shook me, or something."

"I plan to," he said simply. Lifting her tumbled hair away from her face, he briefly touched her cheek.

For the first time in their brief but intense relationship, Julia had nothing to say. Was there something new in his gaze? A tender edge of possessiveness, or a warning of challenge? As if he were officially calling her out, coming after her from here on in with everything he had.

She turned toward the window, lifting the shade. The flight was making its descent through the clouds, which were colored with early-morning light. Their feelings for each other were complicating matters more and more. She had allowed things to go too far last night. It wasn't right. It was only going to make things worse.

An intimate relationship with Storm would be unlike anything she'd ever known. It would be intense, unforgettable. Although Storm obviously wanted to begin an affair, he still didn't want her working with his team. Despite her desire for him, Julia's sense of self-respect simply wouldn't permit her to become involved with him under those circumstances.

Concentration was the key. She couldn't allow her emotions to take hold and cloud her judgment. As she might have advised a client, Julia counseled herself to keep her eye on the ball and steer clear of any more night flights with Storm Donovan.

# Six

——

During the Eagles home stand in Boston Julia felt she was making some progress on both fronts—gaining ground with the team, more importantly, creating some distance from their sexy manager. In regard to the team, her progress wasn't anything to telephone Tokyo about.

Julia discovered Eddie Carlucci seemed to be more on her side than she had suspected. Either that, or she'd simply worn down the coach's guard by hanging around the bull pen, asking a million questions and otherwise making a pest of herself.

The second day back at Fenway, Julia watched as Eddie coached a pitcher on the mechanics of his curveball. During his most recent appearances on the mound, the relief pitcher Gonzalez had trouble hanging the curve over the strike zone. Eddie worked with him on his windup and release for over an hour. Julia stood by, watching, waiting for her chance. As Gonzalez failed to improve much with Eddie's instruction, she could see the coach's frustration mounting. Finally, he called for a break.

"Mind if I talk to him?" Julia asked with deceptive nonchalance.

"Be my guest," Eddie urged her. "Maybe you can whisper in his ear, like you did to Osgood. I'll look the other way a few minutes if you want."

You couldn't straighten out an athlete's form in only a few minutes. But this was more leeway to work with any player than she'd been given thus far, so Julia rushed over to the pitcher to see what she could do.

Luckily Luis Gonzalez liked her. Or at least, liked to flirt with her every chance he had. He looked rather pleased when he saw her coming. Julia greeted him with a bright smile.

In a few minutes, she had engaged him in a friendly conversation, then got him to throw a few pitches for her and all but one pitch was a strike.

Somewhere in his mind, the pitcher knew how to move his body in the perfect form and rhythm necessary to throw strikes. However, now that he'd lost that automatic motion, Eddie's instruction was only making matters worse, Julia thought. For, instead of letting his body take over, trusting himself to find his natural rhythm again, Gonzalez was anxious and self-conscious. He was thinking too much about his mechanics, which was poison for a pitcher.

Before she knew it, Julia had been working with him almost an hour. She instructed him to focus on the strike zone. She told him he'd simply have to try to

forget what his body had to do to put the ball there.
She made him walk from the mound to home plate
very slowly and deliberately, then sit down on home
plate, with his knees folded up to his chest. With his
eyes closed, she asked him to experience the particular space of the strike zone. At first, he thought she
was joking with him. But finally, he got over feeling
self-conscious and tried to get into it.

After he'd pitched some more, she took Gonzalez
through a visualization exercise: she had him picture
himself striking out batters one after another, cruis-
ing with a natural rhythm and a perfect curve.

A little while later, Luis had stopped overstriding.
He had begun to paint the corners of the plate with
four out of six pitches. Eddie walked up beside Julia,
pushing his cap back on his head. Without glancing at
each other, they stood side by side watching Gonzalez.

"I won't say nothing to nobody if you don't," Eddie said in a deadly serious tone. "If anyone asks any
questions, I don't know nothing about how you happened to sneak in some time alone with Luis back
here. Got it?"

Julia's brain did double time working on a transla-
tion. "Got it," she said to her reluctant conspirator.
"Oh, Eddie, one more thing—"

"What's that?" he replied, turning finally to look
at her.

"Thanks," Julia said sincerely.

"Yeah, sure." He looked suddenly self-conscious,
which was exhibited in the way he stuffed a wad of tobacco in his cheek. "You're all right in my book, Ju-

lia," he mumbled around the wad of tobacco. "...Just don't tell nobody I said so," he added.

He pulled down his cap, then walked away, giving the sign to Gonzalez that the workout was over. The pitcher nodded gratefully before he began wiping off his face with a towel. "Is it okay if I walk over and...uh, sit on home plate awhile?" he asked Eddie.

Eddie stared at him, then blinked. "Go ahead I guess, if it makes you feel better," Eddie grumbled. "But if anyone asks you what you're doing out there, say you dropped a contact lens or something."

Gonzalez gestured that he understood as he walked off toward the empty diamond. The last Julia noticed, he was sitting on home plate facing the mound, his knees tucked up to his chest, presumably becoming one with the strike zone.

That night, the Eagles were up against the Pittsburgh Pirates. It was a tough, close game with the Eagles leading by only one run in the ninth inning. They were two outs from victory when the Pirates' batter smashed a double into left field. Fenway's infamous green monster kept the ball in the park. But the tying run was aboard with the winning run coming to bat.

As Julia expected, Storm trotted out to the mound to make a pitching change. He had to call for a right-hander to close it. Whether the manager liked it or not, Gonzalez was the only right-handed relief pitcher available.

Gonzalez came out and took his warm-up throws. The batter returned to the box and Julia held her breath. Gonzalez's first two pitches were low and outside. The count was two balls, *no* strikes. She sat forward in her seat, talking to the pitcher under her breath, urging him to relax and concentrate.

Gonzalez called time; he walked to the back of the mound, then crouched down to pick some dirt out of his spikes. Using her field glasses, Julia thought she could see him closing his eyes, trying to gather his concentration. He stood up again, assuming the set position. Three more pitches were all it took to end the game. The batter watched the first fast curve cruise by, then went down swinging as he chased after the next two.

The fans, including Julia, went wild over the home-team win. Later in the clubhouse she overheard Storm congratulate Eddie on Luis's performance.

"You're amazing, Eddie. One afternoon with you and Luis's got his old stuff back," Storm praised him.

Eddie's glance shifted to Julia, who was standing in the office doorway. "I really didn't do nothing special with him—" he insisted. "You want to talk to Storm, Julia?" he asked politely. "I was just leaving." Suddenly in a hurry, Eddie slipped past her and out the door.

As much as Julia wished Eddie would take her side against Storm, she understood that he was caught in a very difficult position. In fact, seeing how guilty the coach felt taking credit for Luis's improvement, she actually felt sorry for him.

"Haven't we met somewhere before?" Storm greeted her, glibly referring to the way Julia had been avoiding him ever since their steamy, high-altitude embrace. "I never forget...a face," he added as his bold glance took her in from head to toe. "St. Louis, wasn't it?"

"Storm—" Julia crossed her arms over her chest, sighing wearily.

"Somewhere *over* St. Louis I meant to say. Coming back to you now?"

"I just want the statistics on the Astros. Whatever you have available so far. May I have a copy of them, please?"

The high-tech age had arrived in the venerable halls of baseball and there was hardly a manager these days who didn't live and die by his PC. As far as Julia knew, many of them even had two, one in the clubhouse, another terminal in the dugout for those touchy, play-by-play decisions.

An up-to-date analysis of any rival ball club's batting-and-pitching statistics was churned out daily by Storm's personal computer, which was later distributed to the players and coaching staff. Julia didn't see why she wasn't on the circulation list by now.

"I might be able to find a copy," he hedged. "Will you have dinner with me?"

"I ate before the game."

"A drink?" he persisted hopefully.

"Wait a second, let me get this straight. In order to get the stats, I have to go out for a drink with you?" Her gaze narrowed. "That's pretty sleazy, Donovan."

He considered her comment for a moment, his handsome face taking on a thoughtful expression. "Yeah—it is," he agreed. He paused. "So? Do we have a deal?"

"No way," she said flatly. She turned to go.

"Suit yourself," Storm sighed. "I have a nice, fresh copy of them right here—" With her back toward him, she could only hear a sheaf of papers being rattled in a tantalizing fashion. "You could be reading it in bed tonight, Julia. In fact, I wouldn't even mind reading it to you...."

"Keep dreaming, pal." Standing in the doorway, a safe distance away, she turned to face him again.

"Sounds like we'll both have to, Doc. You're the one who talks in your sleep, remember?"

Julia remembered. His direct hit made her blush. But it also pushed her to say more than she'd intended.

"Listen, Storm, if you don't put me on the list for those statistics, it's no big deal. I'll just keep getting hold of them my usual way."

"What usual way?" he asked.

"Nothing illegal. Good night now," she added sweetly.

But the office was small and before she knew it, Storm had a firm grip on her wrist making it obvious that he had no intention of letting her go until she answered him. He gently tugged her back inside, then shut the door.

"My, aren't we macho?" she said, shaking off his hold.

"One straight answer and I'll let you go. What usual way are you getting hold of these reports? Are the guys giving them to you?" he demanded.

"You've got them so brainwashed against me, they wouldn't dare. They treat me like I have the plague.

Like I'm the incredible invisible woman, or something.''

"I only wish you were."

"Can I go now?" If he continued to narrow the field, Julia knew she'd have to pitch her way out of deep water, just like Luis—ninth inning, bases loaded, no outs, face to face with a heavy hitter who could send her into the next galaxy with one kiss.

"Not until you tell me how." He meant business. He was also blocking the room's only exit. Julia decided she had no choice but to come clean. And some perverse little part of her was curious to see his reaction.

"Well—what I do is, I come down to the stadium way before you arrive . . ." She paused. Did she really want to tell him this?

"Go on."

"I come in here, shut the door, then turn on the computer and call up whatever I need. Once I figured out how to access the file, it was pretty easy."

"So, on top of everything else, you're a computer whiz, too?"

"I wouldn't say I was a whiz exactly," Julia replied modestly. Although she'd been pretty proud of herself to so nimbly sneak in and out of Storm's files without him ever suspecting a thing.

"Just enough of a hacker to stick your hand in the cookie jar anytime you like, right under my very nose—"

"More or less, I guess. Yes." Why did he have to make it sound so underhanded? She was only trying to do her job.

"So why in the world did you come in here, asking so politely for a copy when you've been filching the stuff from me, right and left? Talk about sleazy!"

"I wasn't *filching* exactly," Julia defended herself. "I never liked the idea of going behind your back. But what else could I do? I need those stats as much as anyone else on this staff. Maybe more. And you know it."

Coming very close, Storm stared down at her, his expression dark and unreadable. Was she in for one of the famous Donovan Temper Typhoons? It sure felt like something unpleasant was brewing and Julia was tempted to make a mad dash for the door.

"You are the most persistent, pesky, pushy, *ballsy* broad I have ever met in my entire life," he said, his voice rising on every adjective. "And believe me, lady. That's covering a lot of territory!"

He took hold of her shoulders. Julia had no choice but to meet his gaze, her hands coming up against his chest. Instead of looking mad, as she'd fully expected, he wore the expression more of a man totally bewildered.

"Thanks for the compliment," Julia managed in a whisper.

"I didn't mean it as one. I don't know whether to throw you out of here on that sweet bottom..." He paused, his gaze dropping from her eyes to her mouth. "...Or kiss you until the smoke alarm goes off in here."

"Do I have a choice?" Julia's voice was soft, almost breathless. Her hands, resting on his chest, had, for some inexplicable reason, ceased trying to push him away.

"Sorry, Julia," he said finally, "I'm still calling the plays in this outfit."

He pulled her close, then proceeded to kiss her with a hard, hungry passion. Julia felt her willpower sailing over the outfield wall. She seemed to melt against him; as her arms moved up around his broad shoulders, the contours of her body merged and meshed with his in an embrace so intimate it was barely a shade away from lovemaking. She wanted him. No matter what she said or did, her response to his kiss made that truth undeniable.

When his mouth moved away from hers, she felt a bit dazed, instantly missing the delicious pressure of his lips. "Can I see you tonight? I'll stop by your hotel after I finish up here," he whispered softly in her ear.

Julia opened her mouth to speak. "Ye—" she began. Instantly, she caught herself. "Uh, no. I don't think so."

She backed away from him, loosing herself from his grasp.

"Good night, Storm," Julia said for the third time. She turned toward the door.

"Hey, wait." He reached over to his desk and handed her the information on the Astros. "You forgot something."

"Thanks—" Taking the sheets from him, Julia felt completely confused at his behavior. "But I don't get it."

"I have a feeling that even if I padlock this computer, you'll find some way to get hold of them." He shrugged. "Let's just say you scored this one on a fielding error, okay?"

"Sure." Stuffing the papers in her purse, Julia finally left his office and the ballpark.

Back in her hotel room, she took a hot shower. Soon afterward, she called down to room service for some tea and a snack. As Storm had predicted, she got into bed, then began to read over the statistics. She soon became distracted, however, by visions of Storm in bed beside her.

She wondered if hanging on with the Eagles was worth the battle. Tonight she had been a single syllable away from giving in to her attraction for him. Storm could have reacted angrily, or even accused her of being an incredible tease, and he would have every right to at this point, she thought.

But Julia knew she'd honestly never behaved this way with a man before. She had never responded so easily, so completely to any man the way she did with Storm. It was practically impossible to resist him when he touched her. Why couldn't he simply leave her alone? Maintaining a professional relationship was increasingly difficult, and would ultimately disintegrate if she let the intimacy continue.

The Houston Astrodome was the Eagles' next stop. The team's win-loss record had improved slightly over the past two weeks, a small achievement Julia was unable to share in, as she was still forced to maintain her spectator status. The minor improvement was certainly not enough to put them back into the pennant race. However, it was enough to lift the club's spirits, which made her role seem even more superfluous.

Yet, intermittently, she continued to make inroads with the team members. Despite Eddie's request that

Osgood and Gonzalez keep their sessions with Julia a secret, somehow the word got around. Of course, most of the players were skeptical. But one or two others, like the catcher who had witnessed the workout with Gonzalez, were believers. They approached Julia privately to see if she could offer some advice on hitting problems that their batting coach couldn't seem to solve.

The players were still wary of Storm and went out of their way to meet with Julia when they knew the manager wouldn't be around. Storm knew everything that went on with his team—from shaving nicks to lovers' quarrels. Julia doubted that her sessions with these players were really secret from him. Yet, he hadn't tried to interfere. Maybe he figured she couldn't do much damage on such a small scale. When Julia had first met Storm, she had to admit, she smugly thought she could read him like a book. But as their relationship continued, he became more and more of a puzzle to her.

Although the small gains in trust were heartening, they weren't significant enough to really help the team, or to satisfy her. She was getting fed up with sneaking around behind Storm's back in order to simply do her job. She was totally frustrated by her uphill battle with the Eagles. In addition, she suffered a different, more poignant type of frustration in regard to her feelings for Storm. Something had to give.

While in Boston she had learned from Granville's assistant that the team owner would not be back from his trip abroad until the following week. She certainly wasn't going to quit until he returned. Julia decided she would keep chipping away until then. If Storm didn't give her a break by then, she would have to chalk this whole fiasco up to experience. And, as Julia had once heard, experience is what you get when you don't get what you really wanted.

In Houston the Eagles didn't get what they wanted either. The club had come into town with high hopes of taking two or more of the four games they faced with the Astros. Unfortunately, the Eagles lost the first three in a row, which made them drop down to fourth place in the division standings. The third game on Saturday night had been a hard, gritty battle that had lasted almost four hours, stretching on to twelve innings. The oppressively hot weather, so typical of Houston in August, made everyone feel that much worse. Afterward the clubhouse was as quiet as a funeral parlor. The defeat had been demoralizing, and there was still another game to face tomorrow afternoon.

Julia felt so awful for them, she couldn't bear to hang around for the usual wrap-up with Eddie. The defeat brought the past two weeks of frustration to a head. If she couldn't help this squad, she wasn't going to sit by with her hands tied, watching them go down the tubes either.

Back at her hotel, she was too restless and riled up to sleep. She clicked on the TV, ran through the stations and moments later, clicked it off again. The only foolproof method she knew of to alleviate a vile mood was a good, hard workout. Julia decided that despite the late hour, she'd go down and swim some laps in the hotel pool.

The Olympic-size pool had underwater lights; surrounding it were big, lush tropical plants and palm trees. Up above, the night sky sparkled with stars and a low, crescent moon looked as if it had been painted there by an artist's hand. Julia dived in the deep end and felt better instantly. She didn't understand why there was no one else swimming. It seemed the perfect way to cool down on such a hot night.

Determined to tire herself out, Julia began swimming laps at a brisk, steady pace. She'd swum ten and was moving toward the shallow end, when she became aware of someone else diving into the water.

Storm's sleek, dark head popped up about a foot in front of her. She moved to the side of the pool, grabbing on to the wall.

"You shouldn't dive that close to someone swimming laps. I didn't even see you coming."

"Maybe that was the idea. You shouldn't be down here by yourself. It's almost one o'clock in the morning."

"So?" Julia pulled her long wet hair back over her shoulder. Damn the man! Couldn't he give her a moment's peace?

"It's not safe," he insisted, sounding sincerely concerned. "I don't like the idea of you swimming down here all alone."

"You're not *my* manager, Storm," Julia reminded him. "Don't worry, I can take care of myself."

"Sure—you have a black belt in karate, right?"

"Brown—but it'll do in a pinch." He moved toward her. Droplets of water clung to his face and broad shoulders. His dark hair was slicked back, making his rugged features that much more appealing.

"What the heck are you doing down here, anyway? Who the hell goes swimming at one o'clock in the morning?"

"I might ask you the same question," Julia said, trying not to laugh.

"Somebody looking for trouble, that's who," he replied in his typically insistent fashion.

"I'm not going to give you any trouble, Storm," Julia said with a shrug. Just then, the strap of her bathing suit slipped off her shoulder. Before she could reach down to fix it, Storm's hand was there.

"Maybe I plan on giving you some," Storm said, winding his long finger through the fallen strap. He was simply holding on to it where it lay against her arm. The touch of his fingers on her bare wet skin set fires inside her. One false move could mean trouble for both of them.

She was very still, practically holding her breath, trying to anticipate his next move. When Storm dipped his head to alternately kiss and sip at the bare skin just above her breasts, a wave of heat swept through her. He tugged the bathing suit top lower still, working an incredible magic with his lips and tongue that made her body weak with longing. She clung to his shoulders for support while beneath the water's surface, he fit the length of his long body next to hers. He wrapped his arms around her, then pulled her close so that their legs intimately entwined. She could feel his hard, throbbing arousal through the thin material of their bathing suits, which made her weak with longing for him.

The top of her bathing suit had nearly slipped down to her waist. She felt the sensation of the crisp wet mat of his chest hair rubbing against her bare breasts. She ran her hands over him hungrily, over his slick back and down to his slim waist and lean buttocks.

His hand moved down under the water, caressing her bare thigh, cupping her bottom and pulling her up against him. Julia sighed with pleasure as they kissed and swayed together in the water. And Julia knew that every part of her was on fire for him, molten hot and burning out of control. She knew she could go on touching him, kissing him and exploring him all night. Her body craved to be joined with his. The scanty material of her bathing suit, and some lingering recollection that they were carrying on in public, was all that kept her from discovering the unimaginable pleasure of being possessed by him completely.

Storm pulled his mouth away from hers long enough to whisper hoarsely, ''Julia, I want to make love to you—''

''Yes,'' she sighed, letting her cheek fall against his shoulder.

''For hours. For days—'' He pressed his warm lips against her neck. ''Let's go up to your room,'' he said simply, while gently replacing the straps of her bathing suit. She felt his body grow tense against her as he waited for her answer.

Julia framed his beautiful face in her hands. He was easily the most irresistible hunk of manhood she had ever encountered or ever hoped to encounter in her entire life. He was either making her wondrously happy—or absolutely crazy. He filled her thoughts every waking hour and even haunted her dreams at night.

And he was the only man she'd ever known who made her totally lose control, toss her ever-rational, self-controlled method of operation to the wind. No doubt about it, she'd handed the guy a blank check on her, body and soul. Although she knew there were a million practical, serious, sensible reasons why she should get out of the pool and go up to her room alone, Julia couldn't think of one of them.

"Let's go," Julia whispered to him. He looked a bit shocked, as if he didn't quite believe what he'd heard. "*Yes,* Storm," she repeated with a soft smile.

His hands gripped her waist again under the water. "You mind repeating that again?"

"I said, you got the call, pal. Safe at home plate," she whispered against his mouth, imitating the typical ball player's drawl. Lifting herself up, she kissed him softly on the mouth, which was all the assurance he needed.

As they rode up to her room in the impossibly slow elevator, Julia was seized by a shiver of doubt. As if reading her mind, Storm chose that moment to pull her close for another kiss, scattering her doubts again like butterflies.

Alone in her room, she shut the door behind them, twisting the lock. Storm's arms were around her instantly, his kisses slow, lingering and warm as he first eased off the towel she'd wrapped around her. Then he peeled down her wet bathing suit. He was content to take his time, to warm her chilled skin with his mouth and hands, as if slowly stoking a banked fire.

They moved to the bed, as his passionate kisses and caresses, across her neck, her breasts, her stomach and thighs, continued to tease and tantalize her. He covered her mouth with his, their tongues swirling in an intimate dance. His hand swept downward, dipping between her thighs to the source of her honeyed heat. He held her possessively, as he went on with his exploration, stroking her tenderly, passionately. She lifted her hips, urging him on, as she moved rhythmically against his hand. His tender touch, calculated to drive her to the brink, was pure torture but surely the sweetest, wildest she'd ever known.

Deciding to fight fire with fire, she twisted around, until he was lying on his back. She slipped down beside him and ran the tip of her tongue under the waistband of his damp bathing suit. He gasped sharply; his stomach muscles tightened. She pulled the cord at his waist free, then pressed her lips to the curve of his hip bone as she eased his suit lower and lower with her hands. He whispered her name, a sensuous groan of delight, then almost reflexively, twined his fingers in her hair. As she felt his body shudder, Julia was introduced to a new heady sense of power, discovering she could give Storm such pleasure.

She'd never known a man who made her feel the way Storm did, joyful and uninhibited, like a wild thing set free. She wanted to know all of him, to touch him, to taste him, every kiss making her hungry for more. The scent of his skin was like some rare, intoxicating perfume. It coursed through her bloodstream and went straight to her head. She wanted to discover every secret spot that might pleasure him. But the way he returned each of her loving touches made her almost lose track of what she was doing. Moving her mouth languidly across his stomach, then on to his chest with agonizing slowness, she trailed her tongue over one flat nipple, then the other. Her hand swept down over his taut stomach and muscular thighs, finally discovering the hard, throbbing evidence of his desire.

"Ah—Julia. You're driving me wild, honey," he groaned. He put his hands on her waist, pulling her up on top of him. Their mouths met in a deep, soul-shattering kiss; then suddenly, Storm twisted around, taking her with him. She softly landed on her back, staring into his green eyes.

"You're beautiful," he whispered. "You dazzle me. I can't look at you enough. Or touch you. Or kiss you—" His voice trailed off on a ragged sigh as his mouth captured the tip of her breast, sending sweet fire through every trembling inch of her.

Her body ached to feel him inside her, a deep longing to capture him, yet know the sweet satisfaction of total surrender.

"Storm—don't make me wait any longer," she sighed. "I want you so much."

He felt her, warm and ready, restless with longing, burning him with her silken fire. "And I want you. From the very first second I saw you, Julia," he confessed. He moved over her, staring down into her eyes. "I can't tell you how much—" he whispered a second before he made them one.

Julia clung to him, feeling herself shudder at the shock of their joining. They moved together in an ageless rhythm. Julia wrapped her legs around his slim waist, feeling his arms around her, holding her as if he'd never let her go. She knew that making love to Storm was so much more than a physical union of their two bodies. She urged him deeper inside, wanting all of him. And she wanted to give all of herself, to hold nothing back, to surrender, completely.

It was like two stars colliding in the dark and distant night; their lovemaking became explosive. It was the wild north wind, fiercely blowing across mountain peaks, stirring up oceans, gathering a force so powerful that it lifted them up to the sun.

She wished it could last forever. But she knew she couldn't hold off the end a second longer. Finally she felt herself shatter in his arms, sharp and sweet, a crimson spear of light darting through her, leaving her trembling with pleasure again and again in its wake. Storm pushed her still higher, taking her to an unimaginable pinnacle of ecstasy. He felt her tight all around him. His fierce cry of passion was an echo of her own. Then he called out her name—as sweet a sound as Julia had ever heard. And one she'd never forget.

It seemed a long time later when Julia finally opened her eyes. Her cheek resting on Storm's chest, she felt his hand drifting in her hair. "That was beautiful," he sighed. "And you're beautiful. Making love with you is just . . . indescribably fantastic."

"Hmm—you, too," Julia murmured. She knew he'd understand what she meant. She lifted her head to look into his eyes. "So how's your condition?" she asked, dropping a tender kiss on the dimple in his chin. She'd really wanted to kiss that spot for so long. She didn't know why she hadn't gotten to it sooner. "No cold shower for you tonight . . ."

"I don't know—" he replied in a teasing tone. He shifted around, rolling Julia over on her back, stretching out above her. "Strange thing about this condition is, making love to you hasn't cured it one bit, Doc. In fact, I think it's worse than ever.''

"You don't say?" She smoothed her hands across his chest, her fingertips savoring the feeling of his warm bare skin. His hold on her tightened and his passion stirred against her again, causing Julia to move slowly against him in response.

"Oh, I do say, sweetheart," he murmured, lowering his head to press his warm mouth against her breast. "The more I have of you, the more I want," he whispered as her body began to tingle with desire all over again. "Making love to you once was no cure at all."

"Thank goodness—" she sighed. She pulled his head up to hers for a long, deep kiss, telling him with her body and her hands how very much she wanted him, too.

# Seven

Julia woke the next morning to find a sweet note from Storm on her pillow. They had made love all night long, finally falling asleep in each other's arms around dawn. In the note he asked her to meet him down at the stadium for breakfast, so they could have some time alone together before anyone else arrived. She felt warm, recalling the hours of passion they had shared.

Then the shocking reality of the situation hit her and she sat bolt upright. Clutching the note, Julia got out of bed and pulled her robe on. What in the world had she done? "Botched things up beyond repair!" was her answer. How could she continue to stay on with the Eagles after last night? She simply could not. Last night, Storm had been the perfect lover, giving, passionate, revealing to her a wealth of tender feelings for her he'd so far kept hidden. But Julia hadn't fooled herself for a minute into believing that becoming Storm's lover had changed anything in regard to her professional commitment with the Eagles. No, she knew him better than that by now.

And she knew that her own self-respect would not allow her to continue with the team a single day the way things now stood between them. She wouldn't even wait until Granville returned to Boston. She'd pack up and return to San Diego today. Her passion for Storm had cost her dearly, Julia thought, feeling tears come to her eyes. Not only did it force her to give up on the Eagles. But now, after only one night together, she had to turn her back on what might have developed between them. No, she wouldn't allow herself to think about that part of it now. It only made her feel worse.

At the stadium, the door to Storm's office was open. He was waiting for her, sipping a cup of coffee and working on the lineup for the game that afternoon. She stood in the doorway, silently taking in the sight of him, and Julia finally knew what it meant to feel her heart break. Could things ever work out for them, someday, somewhere? Maybe after the season was over. God, she hoped so....

"Hello, gorgeous," he said, getting up to greet her. His smile enveloped her in warmth and affection. "You owe me a good-morning kiss," he playfully reprimanded, as his arms slipped around her. "I mean to collect—"

"Storm—" How was she ever going to get on with what she'd come here to say if she started kissing him? But when their lips met, Julia couldn't resist kissing him back as if they'd been apart for months, instead of just two hours.

Finally she pulled away. "I think we need to talk, Storm," she said.

He felt her grow tense in his arms; his expression became wary. "Uh-oh," was all he said. "Should I brace myself for the old, it was swell, but I'm not ready for a commitment bit? Because I'm telling you right now, Julia—"

Was he going to confess serious intentions about his feelings for her? She partly yearned to hear him say those words out loud. Yet, she knew she couldn't hear him out, then do what she knew she had to.

"No—" she abruptly cut him off. "It's nothing like that. Just hear me out, okay?" she said, trying to gather her thoughts. She moved out of his arms and rubbed her aching forehead with her fingertips. "I'm glad we spent the night together, Storm. It was wonderful . . . perfect, really," she began in a shaky voice. "I don't want you to think I regret anything . . ."

"But?" he interrupted.

"But, because of what happened between us last night, I just can't stay with the team anymore. I'm going back to San Diego this afternoon. It might be different if things were working out. . . . Well, they're not and getting involved this way with you just makes it too complicated for me."

"So you're out of here. Just like that?" he asked, sounding hurt and angry.

"Isn't that what you wanted all along? For me to just leave your precious team alone?" Julia said, feeling hurt, too. Why couldn't he see this from her side for one second? Why was the situation so difficult to understand? "Did you honestly think I would hang around here, having an affair with somebody who was preventing me from doing my job?"

"Slow down a second, will you?" he said, running his hand through his hair. "For crying out loud, you make it sound like I set you up or something."

"Did you?" she asked him point-blank.

"God, Julia—is that what you really think of me?" Her words wounded him. He paced the room in front of her. "I thought you knew me better than that. I thought you—" His voice trailed off and he didn't finish what he'd started to say.

He looked so upset that Julia instantly regretted her words. She was sorely tempted to put her arms around him, to tell him that none of this mattered one bit. If only they could work things out between them.

"You thought what, Storm?" she asked him quietly.

"Nothing. Absolutely nothing." His voice was cold, unyielding. "Right now I'm thinking maybe it's the other way around," he said suddenly, turning to meet her gaze. "What are you trying to do, put the squeeze on me, Julia? Use a little psychology on this dumb jock, put me right where you wanted me all along?"

"What are you talking about?" she asked, backing away.

"You walk in here with this morning-after-regret act and try to twist me around your little finger. I don't think you intend to leave at all. I think you're trying to call my bluff."

"That's ridiculous!" Now it was Julia's turn to feel hurt and betrayed. She hadn't wanted to leave this way, but he'd given her little choice. "I don't play games with people's emotions, Storm," she said turning to go. "I'm sorry you don't understand. I'm only doing what I think I have to."

"Yeah—sure." With his arms crossed tightly over his chest, a belligerent look on his face, Storm watched her walk out the door.

Julia thought for a moment he'd come after her. He didn't. She called a cab to take her back to the hotel so she could pick up her bags. While she waited, she nearly went back up to the clubhouse to tell Storm she'd changed her mind. But she didn't. And Storm didn't come down to stop her from leaving.

He obviously didn't really care about her, she thought. Not the way he'd seemed to last night. It was only his pride that was hurting this morning. He was the type who liked to call the shots with a woman, she guessed. He wasn't used to having someone turn the tables on him.

Julia's mind raced with angry thoughts about Storm and the way he'd turned her life upside down the past few weeks. Soon she was at the airport, ticketed and waiting at the gate for her flight. It was his fault. Entirely. She didn't care if he crawled on his hands and knees to San Diego, she'd never forgive him for accusing her of using him. She'd washed her hands of that fourth-rate, bumbling baseball team of his, too.

Then, for some inexplicable reason, her anger seemed to dissipate and she suddenly started to cry. Big, silent tears first collected at the corners of her eyes, then rolled down her cheeks, falling like raindrops on the open magazine she was pretending to read. She put her sunglasses on to hide her red puffy eyes. What the heck had happened to her? Men never got to her quite like this. Especially one she knew was such an unlikely bet from the very beginning.

"Nice try with the sunglasses, Julia—"

For a moment, Julia thought she was only imagining Storm's voice. When she looked up to see him standing right in front of her, her heart skipped a beat.

"But I wasn't fooled for a second," he continued, as he sat down next to her.

"Too bad. Next time I'll try a fake nose and mustache. What are you doing here?"

"I came to ask if you want to play a game with me—one quick round of Let's Make A Deal."

"Meaning?" Julia asked, while slipping off her glasses and putting them in her purse.

"Meaning what will it take to make you stay?"

Leave it to Storm to surprise her. She'd expected apologies, or even more accusations. But not this. She didn't quite understand him.

"You already know the answer to that question, Storm. I only want to do the job I was hired for, and not on the sly either." There was an announcement that boarding on Julia's flight would begin momentarily and she stood up, reaching for her carryons. "The only way I can help the team is if you get the heck out of my way. And we both know that's never going to happen. You should have saved yourself a trip."

"Wait—" Storm loved a good game of poker. He liked playing for heavy stakes and the moment had come to put his cards on the table. "What if I gave you one man to work on—kind of a test case? And if you're successful with him, I'll get out of **your way** for the rest of the season."

"And if not?"

"If not, you admit it didn't work out. Hopefully there'll be no hard feelings."

"What player did you have in mind for this noble experiment?" She was sure he had some impossible choice picked out for her. Maybe he wanted her to turn a batboy into the next Mickey Mantle.

"Firecracker MacDougal."

"MacDougal? I might have known," Julia sighed.

Firecracker was a brawny, redheaded Georgia peach, thus the nickname. He had a talent for blowing the cover off a baseball with one powerful swing of the bat. MacDougal usually had about twenty home runs a season and often led the league in RBIs—hits that brought other men on base home to score. But the only category Firecracker had been leading the league in lately was strikeouts. In fact, flight attendants and cocktail waitresses were the only moving targets he was hitting on lately with any success at all.

Julia had already observed that the slugger's performance had a big effect on the team's morale and she'd certainly wanted to work privately with him. But he had so far made it very clear that he didn't go in for any of her screwball stuff.

"Now what's the matter? I'm giving you carte blanche to work with the biggest hitter in my lineup. I thought you'd be thrilled, delighted."

"I would be if you hadn't done such a good job of brainwashing MacDougal against me. Not that you had that much to wash," she added dryly.

"I'll talk to him," he promised. "The deal is you get the Cracker's batting back up to the average he had last season."

"And how long do I have to perform this miracle cure?"

"Two weeks."

"Two weeks? That's not enough time—"

"That's the deal, Doc. Take it or leave it. I think I'm being extremely generous."

"Tell the truth, Santa Claus. MacDougal is so far gone, you'd try a witch doctor at this point, wouldn't you?

"I couldn't find any in the yellow pages, so I thought I'd give you a chance," he replied with a smile that made Julia forget why she'd ever walked out on him to start with. "Now, do we have a deal, or don't we?" He stood up beside her, picking up her bags. A bit presumptuously she thought.

"Wait a minute." Julia leaned over, tugging at her bags. "You still haven't told me what's behind curtain number three," she reminded him sweetly.

"Meaning?" She could tell from the glint in his eye that he knew very well she was referring to their personal relationship.

"Meaning the fine print, Storm—you and me, and our mutual, unrequitable condition? I want you to agree that we'll put our…involvement on hold for the next two weeks."

"Or?"

"Or no deal," she said firmly.

"Julia—come on now. Can't we be adults about this?"

"Why start now?" she asked innocently. "Looks like we've got a chance at setting some kind of record here." Boarding on Julia's flight was announced and passengers lined up to have their tickets checked. "Did he just call seats twenty-three to ten?'' she asked, taking out her ticket. "I think that's my section—"

"Okay, okay. Whatever you say. The minute we get back to the stadium, it's hands off for two weeks. Good enough?''

She nodded and offered him her hand to shake. "You've got a deal, Donovan.''

"Great." He took her hand in his, but instead of shaking it, he pulled her toward him. Before she knew it, she was surrounded in a sweet embrace and Storm was sealing their bargain with a smoldering kiss. She resisted for only a second, then couldn't help melting against him, answering his embrace in a way that left no doubt in his mind she was happy he'd come after her.

"I thought we said 'hands off' for two weeks, Storm," Julia said when they finally broke apart. "That wasn't even five minutes ago.''

"I said, as soon as we get to the stadium." Grinning, he picked up her bags and they began walking toward the exit. "That still leaves the cab ride," he pointed out to her.

"True," she said. The look they exchanged silently acknowledged that this part of their bargain was going to be much harder to keep. She wound her arm through his and touched her head to his shoulder. "But it's not a very long ride—"

"Maybe if I slip the driver a twenty he'll be nice enough to circle the airport for a while.''

"Good idea," Julia said, reaching into her purse. She handed Storm a ten-dollar bill. "Here's my share," she said sweetly.

True to his word, Storm had a private talk with the Firecracker before the team's workout. Julia was waiting for him outside Storm's office. When he came out, the slugger looked confused. Julia knew the rest was up to her.

"Storm said you're going to help me with my hitting," Firecracker said, looking none too happy about the idea.

"I'm going to try my best to," Julia replied with a smile she hoped would relax him. He looked nervous, like a little boy who'd been sent out of the classroom for extra help with his schoolwork and was afraid the other kids might make fun of him.

"I guess you singled me out 'cause I'm in the worst hole, huh?"

"Uh—no, not at all," Julia replied, deciding there was no time like the present to start pumping up the slugger's deflated confidence. "I wanted to work with the best player on the team first, the one who needs the least help. You know, get the easy job out of the way. Then tackle the really tough cases."

"Come on—you really think I'm going to be a quick fix?"

He sounded as if he didn't totally believe her, yet part of him, the larger part, Julia hoped, really wanted to. "You been watching me at the plate lately? We're talking serious dead wood," he said glumly, referring to his batting. "I'm in the cellar. I'm eating dirt. I'm so low, lady, down looks like up from here—"

"Yes," Julia nodded, cutting off his laundry list of derogatory metaphors. "I've noticed that. A good sign, too," she added, sounding very upbeat.

"What the heck's so good about it?" he asked, pushing his cap back on his head.

"With this type of problem, a real home-run hitter like yourself usually gets worse before he gets better." This was not entirely a lie, Julia thought. Firecracker couldn't get any worse. He had, as he'd so accurately pointed out, hit bottom and the only way out was up. "I've been watching you very closely and I have a feeling you're going to break out of this slump any day now," she said with a light shrug of her shoulders.

Affirmations of success had to be drilled into Firecracker's mind, over and over again, in order to rebuild his shaky confidence. So often, success or failure was a self-fulfilling prophecy. Julia knew that Firecracker's inner dialogue was an anxious message of self-doubt. If Firecracker started believing he could hit home runs again and kept telling himself he could, he'd do it. Julia was sure of it.

"Piece of cake, huh?" he asked, looking partly suspicious and partly relieved. "How long you think till I bust loose?"

"Hmm, a week," she replied. "Two at the outside." It better be no more than two, she thought, or I'm not just going to be "eating dirt"—I'm going to be eating crow.

Julia had planned to work with Firecracker in a number of ways. Only part of her program for him had to do with coaching him on his mechanics during batting practice. Since this system was most familiar to him and therefore, least threatening or stressful, she'd decided to start there first.

She'd purposely picked a time when there were few other players on the field. Storm had assigned one of the catchers and a pitcher to help her. Julia simply told MacDougal to go up to the plate and swing away.

The results were only slightly better than his performance in a real game. He missed a lot of good pitches, went after too many bad ones. The few hits he made bounced around the infield, which would have produced easy outs for any opponent.

When it was time for a break, he turned to Julia, looking more glum than ever.

"I think I got to pull in my shoulder more," he said, shaking his head. He stared at his bat, then commenced rubbing off a spot of grit, as if it were the sole source of his dilemma. "Maybe if I open my stance?" He lifted the bat up to show her what he meant. "Put more weight on the back leg?"

"Possibly—" Julia said in a guarded tone. Her real purpose had been to observe his level of concentration, rather than his form. He seemed distracted, as if there was a load of static on his mental screen. He was so worried about hitting the ball, he wasn't even seeing it, Julia realized. Her first priority, she knew, was to bring that inner picture into clearer, calmer focus. "I think that's plenty for today."

"You mean we're done?" He looked confused. "Aren't you going to give me some tips for tonight? You know, like keep my big toe pointed at first base—something like that?" he asked eagerly.

He wasn't going to feel relaxed about this unless she told him something, Julia realized. Preferably something that would reduce his anxiety.

"Wait here a minute. I'm going to find you a new bat," she said.

"What's wrong with this one?" he said, holding out the bat in his hand. "You think it's not the right weight or something?"

Bats had to conform to regulation standard and varied only in weight. Usually a big, brawny player like MacDougal liked to swing "heavy lumber."

"The weight is okay. But it doesn't have any hits in it," Julia said with authority. Smiling at his bewildered expression, she walked off the field toward the bat rack in the dugout.

Baseball players were a notoriously superstitious bunch. They were ruled by a hundred and one private little rituals that could bring them good luck or bad. Especially if they were on a streak, or in a slump. Some liked to eat the same exact meal before every game. Some put their uniforms on in a certain order, or had lucky socks or shoes, or even a lucky supporter. Not to mention good-luck pieces hanging in their lockers, or tucked into their pockets during a game. Some said a prayer before they came to bat, and players were known to hum a few bars of a special song. They looked for signs in the universe, a cosmic message that boded ill or well. Whether the national anthem was led that night by a man or a woman. Or if the opposing pitcher's number was even or odd. A ball club coming from a city that started with a vowel could mean trouble. Once they got started, there was no end to it.

Psychologists called this "magic thinking" and though Julia didn't generally encourage the practice, she knew it could often provide a powerful boost to an athlete's motivation. In Firecracker's case, she was willing to pull out all the stops. A little magic thinking applied in controlled doses couldn't hurt at this point, she thought.

A few minutes later, she strolled up to him with a new bat. "Here it is. Don't lose it and don't let anybody else touch it."

He looked it over, searching for some distinguishing difference. If there was one, he couldn't see it. "No one else can touch it, huh?" Now he was looking at her as if he weren't quite sure she was altogether right in the head.

"That's right. One more thing," she added. "When you're on deck, warming up, don't forget to talk to it."

"Talk to it? What the hell about—the weather?"

"About your feelings," Julia said seriously, the idea being that MacDougal's stress could be drastically reduced if he voiced his emotions before coming to the plate, instead of bottling them up. "And a few encouraging phrases," she added, working on regenerating his positive energy. "Just to pump it up, Let it know it has your complete confidence."

He looked down at the bat, then back at Julia. She thought he was about to tell her she was full of baloney, or worse.

"Like 'Nuke this sucker'—that sort of thing?" he asked finally. She smiled with relief. It might help him after all.

"Exactly. And when you're talking to it, picture what you're saying, Cracker. Picture the bat making contact with the ball and sending it out of the ballpark. Got it?"

He nodded. He looked a little embarrassed she thought. But when he walked away, he was holding the bat very carefully. Another player walked by, brushing against him.

"Hey—watch it!" MacDougal said, pulling his new bat out of harm's way.

Firecracker came up to bat four times that afternoon in the last game of the series against the Astros. He struck out, flied out and hit right to the shortstop for a neatly turned double play. Julia watched from the stands, wondering if she had imparted the right advice. The ninth inning rolled around to find the Eagles trailing the Astros by only one run. With two men on base and two outs, Firecracker came up to the plate. He finally made contact—a weakly hit ground ball that hopped, skipped and jumped crazily down the third-base line, somehow eluding capture by the Astros' third baseman and left fielder.

His game-winning hit was not pretty. In fact, some would call it a cheap shot. Bargain brand or not, it allowed two runs to score and saved the Eagles from being swept in the series.

The team poured out of the dugout for high fives, bear hugs and friendly slaps on the backside. MacDougal had come through for them and Julia knew his chintzy hit had been cashed in for a payload of positive reinforcement from his teammates.

# Eight

Back in Boston, Julia was finally given a free hand to work as she was accustomed. Keeping up his part of their bargain, Storm made sure she had the stadium personnel's full cooperation, the necessary equipment and manpower at her disposal.

As soon as they got back to town, she contacted the Eagles' public relations department and met with a video technician to put together a special training tape. Using clips from tapes of various games, Julia made a single reel of Firecracker at the plate, swinging successfully. She also had one of the training rooms in the clubhouse for her own use, where she set up the VCR playback and biofeedback equipment.

The Eagles had a long home stand. Chicago, Montreal and Philadelphia were visiting Boston for the next ten games. Julia knew she had only about that long to put the fire back in the Cracker. There was so much riding on the line—MacDougal's recovery, the Eagles' chance to stay in the pennant race, and her contribution to the club. Not to mention her chance to work things out with Storm. She didn't know what would happen between them during their self-imposed hiatus. She really didn't want to think about it. It was hard enough staying away from him, even for a few days. Two whole weeks seemed a lifetime. But racing against the clock to improve MacDougal's batting average was an ample distraction.

Julia worked with him every day, using all the motivational techniques in her bag of magic tricks; she even came up with a few new ones. Over and over again, Firecracker watched himself on videotape, hitting pitch after pitch out of the ballpark. After days of observation, Julia thought it was not so much a question of correcting some specific problem in his mechanics. And it was not a problem with pulling in his shoulder, or pointing his toe toward the North Pole. His subconscious mind knew the perfect stance, and perfect timing of his swing to get big hits. But for some inexplicable reason he was blocking it out, not reaching a deep enough level of concentration to allow this automatic process to take over.

Julia's first priority was to help him relax, so she taught him relaxation techniques he could use even during a game. Also, before each game, she had him sit alone in the darkened training room and simply stare at a baseball that was backlit by a small lamp. By literally burning the image of the backlit baseball into his mind's eye, MacDougal was better able to pick up the ball during an actual game situation.

In their daily meetings, Julia showed him the videotapes of himself in the right groove and took him through various positive imaging exercises that she hoped would soon trigger something in him that would put the mysterious process of success in motion again.

Of course, the more pitches he hit, the more he believed he would hit. The game-winning hit in Houston was a small but significant start. Every night, Julia watched him from her box seat behind the dugout. Playing against the Chicago Cubs, he had one base hit in each game. That was only three hits for fifteen times at bat, but it was a marked improvement, which picked up his spirits considerably. Even if he wasn't blasting the ball over the outfield wall yet, Julia noticed how the team rallied when MacDougal was on base.

As he started to see light at the end of the tunnel, Firecracker was almost back to his puffed-up, strutting lord-of-the-locker-room self again. Pretty soon he even felt confident enough to give Julia a dose of the infamous MacDougal charm. Using a biofeedback apparatus, Julia was teaching him a relaxation exercise, explaining the point at which one moves from alpha to beta brainwave function.

At first, he was quite cooperative, listening to her instructions. He had stretched out on the training table, and obediently closed his eyes. Julia stood near the table, guiding him verbally through the exercise, while carefully watching the monitor. Suddenly she felt MacDougal's hand moving up her leg. She quickly brushed it off. When she turned, he was grinning at her.

"Can you read my mind with that thing, Doc?" he said.

"It only registers alpha, beta, delta and theta. It doesn't go up to $X$."

Feeling irritated, but not really surprised, she plucked off the connections to the machine from his forehead.

"Unhooking me, huh? That was fast." From his tone, Julia realized he was encouraged by that fact. He sat up, then wound his arm around her waist, forcing her to sit on the table with him. "I got an idea. How about a massage? It really loosens me up before a game—"

"Come on, MacDougal. Stop fooling around," she said, wriggling away. If she didn't take him seriously, maybe he wouldn't take himself seriously, either. "We've got work to do. Do you honestly think I'm going to give you a massage?"

"I meant I want to give you one," he persisted, flashing her a winning smile. "I was visualizing my moves last night," he added, throwing some of her jargon back at her.

Again, he reached for her, but this time she slipped beyond his grasp. The Firecracker had suddenly metamorphosed into an octopus. "Calvin," she said in a calm voice, using his real name, "you are a very attractive young man—"

"Thanks," he said, eagerly hopping off the table. "I think you're a real piece too—"

"Any woman would be flattered by your...interest," she added weakly, managing somehow to keep the table between them. "Especially a woman almost ten years older, like me." The difference was more like six, but Julia didn't mind tacking a few extra innings onto her age if it helped to cool MacDougal's ardor.

"Heck, ten years? That's nothing. I like a woman who's been around the block a few times, know what I mean?"

Never mind the block, she had grown dizzy from playing ring-around-the-table.

"The point is, Calvin, I'm very flattered and I'm very interested in your career. But I think it's best if we're just...buddies. Like being your teammate, okay?"

"I think you have to get to know me a little better. You haven't seen the real me. The real Firecracker. I could put fireworks in your sky, honey—"

"The only fireworks I'm interested in seeing are the kind you make with a baseball bat. Think we can concentrate on that for a while?"

"That's the thing, you've never really seen me in action. I'm going to hit one out of the park tonight, for you," he promised. "Don't believe me, do you?"

"Of course I do," she said firmly. Like it or not, she had to respond positively, or else she'd be undermining the positive thinking that had obviously taken effect. If he misconstrued her interest in him to be personal, she'd have to deal with that later.

He hadn't hit a home run in nearly two months, but he sounded amazingly sure of himself, Julia noticed. She couldn't forget to include this latest motivational twist in the careful notes she'd been taking the past few weeks.

"I think we're finished for this morning in here," she said, ending the session a few minutes early. "Why don't you take some extra batting practice?"

"Good idea. Catch you later." Looking like a kid who had been let out of school early, MacDougal was out the door in no time flat and Julia breathed a sigh of relief.

Seconds after the slugger left, however, Storm strolled in. For the past week she had carefully avoided being alone with him. When she had to update him on MacDougal's progress, she'd pick a time when he was out on the field during the daily workout, or when Eddie or some of the players were in his office.

"I need to talk to you," he said, closing the door behind him.

"I was just going out to watch MacDougal at batting practice. We can talk outside," she suggested.

"No, right here," he insisted. Turning around, he closed the door. Julia didn't know whether to be pleased or alarmed. But Storm seemed to have something more urgent on his mind than breaking their bargain. "People are starting to notice that Firecracker's coming out of his slump," he said, not sounding completely thrilled about the news.

"Wait until tonight. He told me he's going to hit one out of the park." She carefully neglected to add that she was reluctantly the personal inspiration for this effort. Storm would get the completely wrong idea about what had been going on in here.

"He did, huh?"

"Don't you believe him?" Julia replied, coming to Firecracker's defence.

"Oh, I believe him all right. If he said he's going to belt one over the wall, he'll do it. And it's about time, too," he added.

"I still have a whole week with him," she said defensively. "I can't just tap him with a magic wand and have him fall under my spell."

"Why not? You did it to me," Storm added, catching her gaze and holding it.

"You still haven't told me what the problem is," she said, trying to ignore the effect his penetrating look was having on her.

"A few reporters have started asking questions. If he belts one into the ozone tonight, they're going to start asking a lot more."

"So? I still don't understand the problem. You handle the press pretty well from what I've seen." Julia meant it, too. Even when the team had hit rock bottom and reporters had gone after Storm, he had kept his cool, never casting blame on his players.

"I don't want them to find out about you. They'll have a field day with it and the last thing the club needs right now is that kind of distraction. Don't you agree?"

"Oh—I see what you mean, now. You've got a point," she replied. "What will you tell them?"

"The usual—some extra coaching corrected his swing—that sort of thing. Once he starts hitting the ball again, it'll be old news. They'll be on to something else."

Julia thought the persistent ladies and gentlemen of the press that hung around the clubhouse were bound to find out about her role and its relationship to the team sooner or later. But she had to agree that the next few weeks were a critical time for the Eagles. With Firecracker on the yellow brick road to recovery, the team had a chance again. They didn't need reporters in every city hounding them for an inside scoop.

"Do you really think you can keep my work with the team a secret from them forever?" she asked, trying to be realistic.

"Only until we win the World Series." He smiled at her then and Julia felt herself glowing when she smiled back. He looked cheered by MacDougal's progress and the revived hopes for the club. Julia had the satisfaction of knowing she'd helped make it happen.

"After MacDougal hits his home run, let's have dinner together to celebrate," he said, reaching for her hand.

"It's a little early for celebrating, I think," she answered. He brought her palm up to his lips, pressing a soft kiss there. Julia felt her resistance fading. She wanted to narrow the distance between them, put her arms around him, love him. His lips moved down to the sensitive skin covering her pulse. If he didn't stop kissing her soon, Julia knew their hands-off policy was going to be history.

"We still have a whole week left on this...deal. Remember?" she reminded him in a faltering whisper.

"I'm counting down every excruciating minute of it, ma'am," Storm sighed. "I miss you," he said simply. He put his arms around her and she didn't even think to stop him. "I miss talking to you, teasing you. And arguing with you. I miss looking into those beautiful blue eyes," he confessed. "The deal was

'hands off.' You never said we couldn't spend time
alone together—''

She missed him, too. Painfully so. But she wasn't
going to fool herself for a minute that they could have
a platonic evening out.

"We're alone together right now, Storm." She
picked up her wrist to check her watch. "We've been
alone about five minutes. Look what happens."

"So, is this so awful?" He pulled her close, dropping a soft, teasing kiss onto her lips. "Can't we forget about that part of the deal? I think your libido is
arguing a bad call, Julia—'' he teased her.

Their lips met in a hungry kiss, causing Julia to cling
to him. He was right; she wasn't fighting Storm, only
herself. But finally, her logic won out over her emotions, as she managed to pull away.

"I miss you too—" she sighed as she moved out of
his embrace. "But we agreed on two weeks. A deal is
a deal."

"Why? I don't get it."

"I still think being involved with you while I'm
working with the team is a conflict of interest. I want
you to honor my decision."

Storm looked frustrated and confused, but she was
relieved to see he wasn't angry. "Okay, the deal sticks.
But when the clock runs down, you'd better know
what you want, Julia."

Julia didn't know what to say. The truth was, from
the moment she'd met Storm she had *known* what she
wanted. The question remained whether or not her
professional ethics would wind up taking a back seat
to her desire.

As promised, Firecracker sent one out of the park at the top of the sixth inning. The roar from the crowd was deafening. The slugger rounded the bases with a slow trot, savoring his big three-run homer. There could be no doubt that Firecracker MacDougal was back in business. The Eagles moved ahead of the Montreal Expos by a score of 4-2, holding on to that edge to win the game.

Storm closed the clubhouse to reporters, having already asked the PR director to field questions about Firecracker's revival. Julia thought it would be best to leave the stadium right after the game and go directly to her hotel. She returned to her room just in time to see Firecracker's home run replayed on the late news. When a shot of Storm's joyful response appeared on screen, she realized that she could have been with him right now, celebrating, instead of facing a hot cup of tea and a cold empty bed. For a smart woman, Julia, she told herself, you're really stupid sometimes.

Although she thanked Firecracker warmly for the home run, Julia managed to talk him out of trying to *score* in any other ways with her. He was too absorbed with breaking out of his slump to be disappointed for long.

In the next three games against the Phillies, he continued to terrorize the opposing pitchers. His average was swiftly rebounding to its prior status and his noisy bat had wakened the entire Eagles' bench. The Eagles were suddenly winning more and losing less and were just a few wins short of tying the Pirates for second place.

Charles Granville finally returned from the Far East, just in time to attend the last game against the

Phillies. Afterward, he invited Julia and Storm to dine with him. They managed to agree beforehand that until their private bargain had been settled, they would keep up appearances for their employer, pretending that Julia's work with the team was going smoothly.

After their series with Philadelphia, it was on to New York, where the Eagles would play the number-one team in the East, the Lions. But the Eagles didn't seem rattled by the prospect. In fact, on the bus to the airport Friday morning, spirits were high; they talked tough about blowing the Lions out of their own park. And eventually, out of first place.

Julia anticipated the trip to New York with a mixture of joy and dread. After the three games in New York, the deadline on her deal with Storm would be up. Julia knew she'd fulfilled her end of the bargain in regard to Firecracker. But she was still in a quandary over her feelings for Storm.

The first two days in New York, she managed to avoid him. It wasn't all that difficult. In her free hours she stayed away from the stadium, shopping and even visiting a museum or two. Storm was totally absorbed managing the team, going over the lineup a thousand times, seeing to every small detail that might contribute to beating the Lions. The Eagles, unbelievably, won two in a row from New York. The club was so excited about the prospect of winning all three, Julia wondered if Storm had forgotten their agreement.

It was Firecracker's birthday and the Eagles were throwing him a surprise party after the final game against New York. Julia was pleased when one of the players invited her. Although the press was unaware of the role Julia had played in the team's comeback, the staff and players certainly weren't. She had earned a place with them and was no longer treated as an unwelcome outsider.

Against all odds, the Eagles beat New York for the third time in a row on Sunday afternoon. Once again, Firecracker had pulled through with big hits at crucial moments. The Eagles three-game sweep had moved them into second place. But the locker room sounded as if they'd won the World Series. The only thing missing was the champagne, and they looked forward to that part at MacDougal's surprise party.

As Julia zipped up a brand-new black linen dress she'd bought at Saks Fifth Avenue, she was seized with a bad case of pre-party jitters. Feeling a mixture of anticipation and dread, she stepped into new shoes, then sprayed on some new perfume. A saleswoman had warned her to wear it, if she was prepared to face serious consequences. When she brushed out her long hair, she had to admit that she looked darned good and thought Storm would think so, too.

There was always the possibility that Storm had lost interest in resuming a relationship with her. But if she really believed that, she would not have bothered with the new dress, not to mention the new lacy, black lingerie underneath it.

There was a sharp knock on the door and Julia nearly jumped out of her skin. "Just a second," she said, walking to the door. When she pulled it open Storm was standing there.

"Oh—hi," was the only brilliant greeting she could come up with. He looked impossibly handsome, wearing a navy-blue suit, stark white shirt and a red silk tie. She wondered if he always dressed up like this when one of his players had a birthday. And who were the flowers for—Firecracker?

"May I come in?" He grinned.

"Uh—sure." She stepped aside, let him in, then factored a quick mental equation—Julia plus Storm, alone in a room with a queen-size mattress . . .

"These are for you," he said, handing her the bundle. "They're roses," he said, noticing her baffled expression when she peeled back the green tissue paper, revealing long-stemmed buds.

"Gosh, thank you . . . but how did you know I love white ones?"

"You told me, silly. That night we had dinner in San Diego. Remember the roses on the terrace?"

"Oh—of course. Let me put these in some water." There was a vase on the dresser that contained an arrangement of silk flowers. It wasn't perfect, Julia thought as she emptied it, but it would do.

She remembered the roses that night, but was amazed that he had. His thoughtfulness was very touching. Especially when she considered how totally absorbed he'd been the past few days with his gang of zany ball players.

"I really hate to be late for surprise parties," she said, placing the vase on the dresser and picking up her purse. "Shall we go?"

"Let's not," he suggested. "You look too beautiful to share tonight. Let's have our own party."

"Storm—" She didn't know what to say. So, that was why he showed up here so early with an armload of roses. It was making sense now. "If you think we're going to just lock the door and hop into bed—"

"Now there's a good suggestion. But I don't want you comparing my seduction technique to that of an amorous baboon again. My plan for the evening is a little more civilized, dinner in Manhattan, dancing, a carriage ride through Central Park. A few distractions to fill up those long hours between now and midnight, Cinderella."

"Oh—so you're willing to go the distance on this, huh?" she teased him. He didn't want her final answer, just a few hours alone so he could remind her how good they were together. As if she needed any reminding.

"Let's just say that before you give me your answer, I want to pitch you my best stuff."

"Managing this one by the book, are you?"

"You've seen my work. I don't take chances in the late innings. So, what it'll be, MacDougal's surprise party, or mine?"

Was there a woman alive who could have refused him? If there was, Julia knew she wasn't the one in ten million. She walked toward him, got up on tiptoe and kissed his cheek. It was so smooth, he must have shaved twice. He smelled great, too. She heard his sharply drawn breath, but he didn't try to hold her.

"That was for the roses, Donovan. Now, let's get out of here, before we forget about the rest of your civilized good intentions."

Storm really had given quite a bit of thought to his private surprise party. Julia was impressed. First by the limousine that was waiting outside the hotel with a chilled bottle of champagne and real crystal flutes on the bar in the spacious rear compartment. She also wondered how he'd ever managed to reserve their own private corner upstairs at an exclusive restaurant. When Storm threw a party, cost was clearly no object. However it wasn't his extravagance that impressed her. He could have brought her daisies and taken her to a burger joint. It was his wholehearted effort to make her happy while they were together that Julia found so touching.

Naturally their dinner conversation soon turned to the Eagles and the sudden upswing in their fortunes. "I have to admit, Julia, tossing you MacDougal was really a desperation maneuver on my part. I never thought you'd turn the guy around."

"So why did you do it?" she asked, gazing at him over her wineglass.

"I knew I had to do something, or you'd have really walked out on me."

She hadn't realized up until now how much he'd wanted her to stay. "So your gamble paid off," she said.

"I wish." He smiled, taking her hand. She knew he wasn't talking about the ball club any longer. He was wondering about their relationship. "I'm still waiting to see how this one turns out. Any inside tips on the matter?"

When she was alone with him like this, Julia couldn't think about the complications of an affair with Storm in a rational way. She couldn't reason at all. Yet, she wasn't quite ready to give him any real answer yet.

"Umm—just one," she replied, winding her fingers through his. "If you promise a lady dinner and dancing, it's bad form to forget the dancing part."

"I didn't forget," Storm replied, squeezing her hand. "I've been looking forward to putting my arms around you all night."

The way he looked at her made Julia's pulse race. She had a sudden impulse to whisper that they could skip the dancing altogether if he liked. But if Storm could stand it a few hours longer, she decided she could, too.

After dinner, Storm took her to an elegant club in a Greenwich Village brownstone. The music, a mix of jazz and old blues standards, seemed to suit their mood perfectly. It was heaven to have Storm's arms around her again, Julia thought, as they moved together on the dance floor in perfect time, barely exchanging a word for the longest time.

The pianist had just finished playing one of Julia's favorites, "It Had to be You," when Storm lifted her face to his and kissed her. "Twelve o'clock, Cinderella," he whispered. "Time to leave the ball."

She looked up at him, nodding in agreement. She knew they had to talk, yet she couldn't say a word. They left the club and got into their limousine. Storm pulled her close and kissed her again and again. "I feel like I've waited two lifetimes for you," he whispered, "instead of two weeks."

"Storm—I want to be with you, too—" Julia touched his face with her hands, letting her fingers drift through his thick hair. "—But I'm confused," she whispered finally. "I'm afraid."

"What are you afraid of?" he asked softly. "Compromising your professional reputation? You're also allowed to have a life, you know—"

"I know," she sighed. "It's not only that—" If word got out that she and Storm were romantically involved, it certainly wouldn't help her professional image. Then again, this wasn't just some superficial fling. It was a once-in-a-lifetime feeling with a once-in-a-lifetime man. It was serious—at least for her.

"What then?" he asked patiently.

"There's the team to consider. I'm not sure it would be good for their morale. Especially now, when they've just started accepting me."

"Well, they'll all be jealous of me, that's for sure," Storm said, kissing her nose. "But maybe that'll fire them up on the field. Just have them visualize my face on the baseball," he suggested.

"Storm—I'm serious," she said.

"So am I." He did sound serious, too, all of a sudden. He pulled away only slightly and Julia acutely missed his close warmth. "Julia, I can't talk you into something you don't feel right about. I honestly don't want to."

"What does that mean?"

"It means, I think you're trying to tell both of us that your answer is no."

"I never said that—" she replied softly.

"Maybe you don't have to." He sighed. "Listen—I know when to give up. You can stay and work with the team for the rest of the season. I won't bother you."

He still had his arm around her shoulder but Julia felt as if they were miles apart. They were quiet for a long time, the bright lights and traffic passing by as the limousine carried them uptown to their hotel.

"I guess I'm just afraid, Storm," Julia said finally. "Of my own feelings more than anything else." She was afraid that she would fall in love with him—maybe she was *already* in love with him. When you loved somebody the way Julia knew she loved Storm, it was like letting that person lead you blindfolded to the edge of a cliff.

"I know you're apprehensive, Julia," Storm said finally, "but don't you think I feel the same way about you?"

"You do?" She honestly didn't believe she could have the same power over him that he had over her.

"Why do you sound so surprised? When I met you that first day in Granville's office I think that's why I was so awful to you. I knew I wanted you from the start, but you were out of my league. The kind of woman who'd never get seriously involved with a guy like me. But here we are, a plenty long shot, as they say. Maybe we've got to just close our eyes and take a chance."

Storm drew her close again. Julia surrendered to his embrace without answering him. She couldn't fight her feeling anymore. When she was in his arms like this, she didn't even want to. For once in her life, Julia didn't try to logically predict what the future would bring. She didn't know how long her affair with Storm would last, or what problems might arise. She only knew that in her heart the passion she felt for him made their time together well worth the risk. Maybe they were a long shot, but one she was willing to put everything on the line for.

A few minutes later, standing outside her hotel room, Julia watched Storm turn the key and open the door. At that very moment she knew deep within, that she was crossing a new threshold. For Julia, this was a new beginning—the start of something grand and mysterious, even a little frightening. Her musings were interrupted by the sound of the door closing in the darkness. Then, Storm's arm wrapped around her and pulled her to him, Julia knew this night with Storm would mark the start of a whole new phase in her life. She had been involved in serious relationships before, but had never known the depth of commitment she now felt with Storm. It didn't matter one bit that they had never really talked about love, or the future. She felt a deep, unshakable sense that a pledge existed between them nonetheless. A commitment to a long, wonderful journey they were about to embark on together.

As they kissed and touched in the darkness, the heat rising between them, Storm's clothes seemed an intolerable hindrance. He had already shed his jacket, after which Julia made short work of his tie. She had begun unbuttoning his shirt, and when she finished there, she moved deftly on to his belt buckle. She parted his shirt and rubbed her cheek and hands against his hard chest, branding his cool skin with her kisses. As her tongue swirled around one flat male nipple, she felt his big body shudder in her arms. Her lips wandered lower, covering his tight abdomen with kisses. The sound of him sighing on her name made her feel deliciously sexy, hungry to taste every part of him.

Somehow the zipper on her dress had been pulled down. The expensive new purchase slipped from her shoulders, then down into a wrinkled heap on the floor. Julia had almost forgotten about the daring black lace camisole she'd worn tonight. Storm sud-

denly halted their embrace, then stepped back to get a
better look, which abruptly reminded her.

"God—you are gorgeous—" An instant later his
arms were wrapped tightly around her again and she
soon found herself lying beneath him on the bed.
"Gorgeous, and all mine," he whispered huskily.

The remainder of Storm's clothes soon joined the
pile on the floor, giving Julia full access to the man
who was now gazing down at her. She savored the
feeling of his bare skin next to hers. Their legs inter-
twined intimately as Storm's warm mouth swept
across her bare shoulder, then lower to her breast. He
slipped the ribbon slim strap of her camisole with his
fingertip, teasing her to distraction as he traced the
edge of black lace with his tongue, his moist mouth
swirling around the crest of her breast, coming close,
but not quite covering the tingling hard peak. Julia
moved restlessly against him, her hands sweeping
across the hard muscles on his back. The hard, hot
evidence of his desire pressed against the sensitive skin
of her inner thigh, forcing Julia to let out a soft moan,
feeling herself melt inside with longing for his complete possession.

Finally, his mouth seized the hardened tip of her
breast, his erotic assault sending shivers of heat
through her body. Julia sat up abruptly then, pulled
the teddy up and over her head, tossing it aside. As
their mouths clung together once more in a feverish
kiss, Storm cupped her bottom in his hands and rolled
over onto his back, bringing her with him. His hands
swept down her smooth back, sliding in at her waist,
lovingly molding the flare of her hips. Arched over her
lover, Julia continued to kiss and caress him, her

breasts tingling as they rubbed against the hair on his chest. He moved his body against hers, the silky core of her femininity pressing urgently toward his manhood.

"Feel how much I want you, love? How much I need you?" he whispered, his hips moving with a maddening rhythm, hinting at the fiery ride that was yet to come.

Julia knew her need for him was just as deep, just as intense. Her body was primed, aching for their joining. Instead of answering him with words, she showed him how much she desired him, her mouth sliding down his strong throat, as her legs tightened around his hips. She ached to be one with him and shifting her hips ever so slightly, she thrilled at the shock of his entry.

He moved inside of her slowly at first, drawing out each powerful stroke of his passion. Julia felt her whole being open to him, her body, heart and soul. There was no place within her now left untouched by the pure, white fire of their love. Moving with Storm, faster and faster, she felt as if she were becoming part of all he was. Now she felt so close, so secure, so passionately joined to the man she truly loved. They moved together in a place beyond time, where their compelling passion for each other encompassed the entire meaning of their existence.

But, just when she thought she couldn't stand the intensity of her pleasure another second longer, she felt as if she'd been hurled over the edge like a shooting star, her body shimmering in waves of a sensual explosion. She clung to Storm's hard shoulders as he continued to move inside her. Peak after peak of searing pleasure made her tremble in his arms. Seconds later, she heard him call her name as his body tensed beneath her, shuddering with the climax of his passion.

Wrapped around each other, they lay quietly for a long time. Julia could feel Storm's uneven breath gently fan her cheek. He raised his head to rain soft kisses on her closed lids, her cheeks and lips. She slowly opened her eyes to see his precious face so close to hers on the same pillow.

"You're the best thing that ever happened to me, Julia," he said in an uncharacteristically serious tone. "Please don't ever forget it."

Julia was so deeply touched by his words and the tender look in his eyes, that she could barely speak.

"I won't," was all she could say. She hugged him closer, tucking her head beneath his chin, her cheek pressed to his warm chest.

"I won't let you," he promised. Then, sealing his pledge, he kissed her. Julia reciprocated, kissing him deeply, feeling herself come alive once more at his touch, as he drew her close. She wrapped her arms around him, amazed at how she could never seem to get enough of his lovemaking. After tonight she felt positive that she never would.

# Nine

___

"These guys are on a streak. They're hot. They're red hot; they are smoking—" Eddie was talking to Julia so fast and the din in the clubhouse was so loud, she could hardly keep up with his words. She just kept nodding, wondering if and when he was going to run out of steam. "—You got to love it. Know what I mean?"

Julia nodded some more. She did love it. In her own quiet way she felt as elated as Eddie sounded. The Eagles had just plucked the Cardinals clean in three games out of three and they had done nearly as well a few days before in Cincinnati against the Reds.

The club was on a winning streak, which meant their spirits were at an all-time high. With every victory they chipped away at New York's first-place standing. With every passing day, Julia knew the decision she'd made to stay on with the team and continue her relationship with Storm had been the right one. The only one, really.

Though Storm was hardly the man she'd imagined for herself, he was turning out to be everything she'd ever wanted. At times, the bond was so strong between them she was sure that Storm possessed the other half of her soul.

Somewhere between their rocky start in San Diego and Firecracker's miracle cure, it had become more important to Julia to help the Eagles because of Storm than to prove she could stick it out. Loving Storm had changed her. He had given her back a part of herself that had been walled off, hidden. No matter what happened between them, she would be grateful to him for that.

After Firecracker, many of the players with hitting problems sought Julia out for advice. She was finally free to work with the team as she had always wanted—not confining her efforts to one "test case" or sneaking around behind Storm's back. She worked with players on individual problems, and also met with the team as a group, for special motivation exercises.

Storm didn't pretend to understand how it had happened. But he wasn't going to deny anymore that all her talk about positive imaging, right brain or left, really worked. Contrary to his fears, Julia's efforts didn't seem to affect his influence with the players at all. Or, if he thought so, he hadn't made an issue of it.

"What an idiot I was to make things so difficult for you," he told her one night when they were curled up together in bed. "The club could never have come back this strong without you, Julia. And I was such a first-class jerk, I almost chased you away.''

"Second class, maybe. Not quite first," she replied, smiling into his eyes. He had been impossible all right, but come to think of it, so had she. "I rated first class, keeping us apart for so long. Thank goodness you wouldn't take no for an answer.''

"You'll never chase me away," he said, nuzzling her shoulder with soft kisses. "Like it or not."

As they kissed and held each other close, Julia silently prayed his words had been true. She'd been aching to tell Storm that she loved him, but she was afraid that maybe it was too soon. Too much for him to think about right now.

He hadn't told her yet that he loved her, but Julia didn't worry about hearing the words. When they were together, he told her in a thousand different ways how deeply he cared for her. Julia didn't press him for more.

Right now, their first priority was getting through the season and hopefully, getting into the World Series. Even their relationship took a back seat to that. For now, Julia was content to enjoy what she had with Storm, one day at a time without worrying about their future.

Right after the team left New York and played Cincinnati, Julia was included in the meetings Storm held with his coaching staff. At first, she felt out of her element. She planned to listen and say little until she felt comfortable in the high-pressure strategy session. She was almost the last to arrive and sat down next to Eddie. The batting coach, Sam Belcher, and the third-base coach, Willie Tucker, greeted her with a what-the-heck-are-you-doing-here look. They appeared to be bracing themselves for the moment when Storm came in, chasing her out.

Storm arrived, then began handing out his statistical information. The staff started the task of reviewing the Eagles' lineup for the upcoming game. The Reds were going to start a pitcher named Dobson, known for his fastball. Belcher made a few suggestions about having certain players shuffled around in the batting order.

"Valentine can hit Dobson," he said, referring to the third baseman, "but he's been in a slump—0 for 15 in the last series. I think you should put Russo in at third."

"Russo for Valentine, huh?" Storm looked at his lineup sheet, then flipped through some other pages of statistics, checking Russo's average and his hitting record against Dobson, Julia assumed.

Julia had been working with Valentine. She didn't think her opinion would count much in the meeting, not when hers was going against Belcher's, who'd been in major-league ball for about thirty-five years. But never one to hold her tongue, she spoke up.

"I think you should leave Valentine in, Storm," she said. "If you put him on the bench, I think his dry spell will get even worse. Why not play him tonight when he has a good record against Dobson? He'll probably get in at least one solid hit. It might turn him around."

"She's got a point. Let him hit his way out of it," Willie Tucker said. Beside him Belcher grumbled, but nothing Julia could translate into words. "Hey—I just call them the way I see 'em, pal," Willie added, turning to the other coach.

"Let's go over the rest of it. We'll get back to the Valentine business later," Storm suggested, moving on to discuss the Eagles' pitching. "We've got Osgood starting tonight. How does he look, Eddie?"

"The hanging curveball is working like a charm. He's feeling pretty up after the New York game," Eddie added.

"Up? Or too up?" Storm asked, sounding concerned.

As Julia knew, there was a certain adrenaline level that would give a player maximum performance. Below or above that level they wouldn't be working most efficiently, failing to reach a proper level of concentration. When it came to psyching up, a rookie like Wally was more prone to boiling over like a pot on too high a flame.

"Well—" Eddie hedged, "it's hard to tell. The kid's such a bundle of nerves normally, how do I know when he's too pumped up?" Storm frowned. He hadn't liked Eddie's answer. It was Eddie's job to know. "He talks to Julia. Maybe she knows how to read him," Eddie offered, giving the floor once more to Julia.

"Well?" Storm tapped his pencil on his clipboard, while looking at Julia. "What do you think?"

"I think he'll be okay," she replied. "I can go down to the bull pen and do a relaxation exercise with him after he warms up. That should help."

"A relaxation exercise?" Storm didn't look very reassured.

"You know, help him with his breathing," Eddie cut in. "I've seen her do it with him. It really settles him down."

"Oh—the breathing thing…" Julia could tell Storm was remembering her first game with the club in San Diego and how he had caught her red-handed working with Osgood in the bull pen. "Okay, let's go with the kid. No sense messing up the whole rotation. But he'd better learn how to put a lid on himself before we go into postseason play."

Julia was pleased to hear Storm refer to the play-offs and World Series in such a positive, matter-of-fact tone. He really believed the Eagles would make it. So did she.

The rest of the meeting was devoted to defensive strategy, how the outfielders would shift over—put the shift on—or move deeper into the outfield when certain Cincinnati hitters came to bat. There were other strategical fine points to discuss, that Dobson was an easy pitcher to steal a base from, for example. When the meeting was over, the coaches left to work with the squad. Julia felt she was finally on the inside track, that her observations and opinions had been seriously considered.

The more she attended the meetings, the more readily she offered her ideas. Not every suggestion was a gem, or necessarily followed through. But, because of the special way she worked with the players, Julia had a unique insight into their strengths and weaknesses. Besides, it was hard to argue with success. For the most part, Julia's ideas had successful results. By the time the team returned home to Boston from St.

Louis, even the crusty Sam Belcher was willing to consider her opinions.

She hadn't the slightest clue that her input into the team's management was beginning to grate on Storm's nerves until one night when they were having dinner. They'd been back in Boston about a week. After losing an afternoon game to the Dodgers, Storm took her to his favorite Italian restaurant.

"Just playing against Lasorda makes me hungry for linguine," he said, looking over the menu. Tom Lasorda, the manager of the Dodgers, was as famous for his love of Italian cuisine as his colorful managing style. "We should have come here last night, for luck," he said.

"Is linguine luckier with red clam sauce, or white?" Julia teased him, looking over her menu. "Maybe we should give each player a strand to put in his pocket for tomorrow night."

"We shouldn't have lost today," Storm said glumly. "We gave that game away. I can't believe Stubbs missed that easy fly ball in the third inning," he said, lamenting the catching error that allowed two runs to score. "Maybe he needs a seeing-eye dog out there."

"Why don't you put Jenkins in center field tomorrow and let Stubbs play Friday, against the left-hander?"

"Good idea," Storm glanced at her briefly over the top of his menu. He was still frowning, but Julia knew the loss had upset him.

The Eagles had been playing well during their home stand. Now, they were only five games out of first place. Losing one game to the Dodgers was not really crucial. But with the season drawing to a close, every game was important.

"I think you could move Valentine to shortstop and put Russo on third. He has better concentration lately, he's quicker guarding the line," Julia mused. "With Randy Hunt pitching, there are going to be a lot of ground balls hit toward left field—"

"You don't say?" Storm replied dryly, taking a sip of his red wine. "Maybe you'd like to suit up and play first base?"

"Maybe Friday," she said, crunching down on a bread stick. "I don't hit that well against righties," Julia teased.

He was tense, touchy and hungry, Julia told herself as she forced herself not to overreact. She'd be a model of patience and understanding. He'd feel sorry about this later. He'd better.

"You didn't happen to discuss this sparkling analysis with Belcher or Tucker, did you?"

"Possibly," She shrugged. "Why do you ask?" Although Storm's voice was calm, Julia felt a knot in her stomach.

"Because Russo was working out at third base and Valentine at shortstop this morning, that's all."

"Oh." Julia didn't know what to say. "Maybe they had the same idea," she said finally.

"Well, it sure would be nice if someone told me about it. I feel like I wandered into that old Abbott and Costello routine, Who's on first? What's on second?" Storm grumbled.

"Storm, calm down. You're getting upset over nothing."

"I don't call it nothing when your coaches forget who the manager is."

"What's that supposed to mean?" Julia didn't want to start an argument, but there was obviously more to Storm's bad mood than losing to the Dodgers.

"It means that lately, I'm starting to feel like my contract has been canceled. The problem is nobody told me. My coaching staff doesn't even come to me with their problems anymore, they go straight to you."

"Storm, stop. That's not true," Julia insisted. "You're exaggerating."

"Really? This isn't the first time this has happened. What about last week, when Witoski's elbow was sore?" he said, mentioning a problem with one of the starting pitchers. "Did Eddie come to tell me first, or you?"

"You're being silly now," Julia couldn't deny that what he said was true, but he wasn't being fair. "I happened to be the first person he ran into, that's all. He would have told anyone about it. The man who picks up the laundry—"

"You know what I'm saying is true, Julia. This is exactly what I was afraid of. Everyone's getting confused. I'm losing my clout."

"For goodness' sake, you make it sound as if I'm trying to steal your job," Julia said. Enough was enough. She was really upset and no longer willing to put his feelings before her own. "Is that what you really think?"

"Of course not—"

"Well you're sure putting a pretty good case together for it."

"I'm not blaming you . . . exactly," he said, taking a deep breath. "Listen, I'm sorry I even brought it up. I guess I feel edgy after the loss. You're probably right. I'm making a big deal out of nothing."

"It isn't nothing, Storm," she said, trying to understand the situation from his point of view. "But does it really matter which of us says what's on first and who's on second, as long as the team keeps winning?"

"They have been winning," he agreed, a slow smile coming to his lips.

"Besides," Julia added, covering his hand with hers. "I hope you realize I'm sticking around to help this bunch of social misfits for one reason, Donovan—"

"The glamor? The excitement? The witty, intellectual conversations in the locker room?" To each joking guess she shook her head a definitive "No."

"Because I love you, stupid," she whispered. As soon as Julia had said the words, she realized that it was the first time she'd actually said them out loud to Storm. She'd grown so accustomed to the idea in her own mind, it had just slipped out.

"Is that a fact?" Storm's smile was dazzling. He was speechless for a long moment. Julia didn't even take a breath. Then he simply got up from his chair, leaned over toward her and kissed her, taking her breath away. "I love you, too. I didn't know I could love anyone as much as I love you—" His words trailed off as he kissed her again, this time quick and hard. Then he abruptly stood up from his chair, then pulled Julia up with him. "Let's get out of here," he said, tossing some bills down to cover the check.

"What about dinner?" He scooped up her belongings, took her hand, and started walking toward the door.

"Room service," he said simply. "Later."

Julia considered the change in plans for only a few seconds. "Good idea," she agreed. "I think the kitchen stays open till two a.m."

The Eagles won two games from the Dodgers and lost two. During their next week at home, they played the San Diego Padres and the Houston Astros. Julia tried to keep a low profile, deferring to Storm when big issues were tossed in her lap by players or even the coaching staff. Storm didn't bring the issue up again. But she could tell that he continued to be silently aware of each situation that justified his side of the argument. The team kept playing great baseball. Even in close games, the Eagles seemed to be getting all the breaks, making the impossible catches and capitalizing on the other team's mistakes.

September arrived, the month when pennants were clinched. The Eagles left Boston for their final road trip against the West Coast teams. They were still five games behind New York, but the Lions seemed to be losing steam. Every time they lost, the Eagles gained a little more ground.

The Eagles did well against Chicago, Los Angeles and San Diego. Their wins, combined with New York's losses, put them only two slim breaths of a game away from first place by the time they arrived back in Boston almost two weeks later. They were so close they could taste it. Coincidentally enough, the next team visiting Fenway was in first place—but not for long the Eagles hoped. The team to beat was the New York Lions.

Reporters on the sports beat had been paying more attention to the Eagles lately. Now that there was a division title at stake and a spot in the National League play-offs, the club's reincarnation had become a story of national interest. When the team plane touched ground at Logan airport, the press was out to greet them in force. It looked as if they had come up in planeloads from New York, not to mention the usual local crowd.

The next day at the stadium, Julia remarked to Eddie about the unusual number of reporters hanging around the clubhouse.

"Better get used to it," he said. "These guys are going to be on us like white on rice if we make it to the play-offs. Even if we don't," he added knowingly, "there'll be plenty hanging around for the death rattle interviews."

They did look predatory, Julia observed. Recalling her discussion with Storm a few weeks ago, she tried to avoid the reporters completely. If they noticed her at all, they didn't seem to think she performed a role of any great importance with the club. Maybe they thought she was the club manicurist, she mused, or Storm's personal secretary.

The Eagles had to win three games out of the three against New York in order to capture first place in the Eastern division. They won the first two easily and came back from six runs behind in the eighth inning to win the last. It was their biggest moment of the season so far; even Charles Granville was down in the clubhouse after the victory to offer his congratulations all around.

When Julia and Storm got back to Storm's apartment very late that night, they fell on the bed in an exhausted, happy heap, quickly falling asleep in each other's arms. Julia woke up the next morning to the sound of Storm's off-key baritone in the shower. She pinned up her hair, pulled back the curtain and joined him. His singing was soon replaced by deep sighs of desire as they began celebrating their private holiday in their own private style.

Back in the bedroom, they held each other afterward. Storm twisted around, pulling Julia up on top of him. "You know something? I'm one lucky son of a gun," he said merrily. "Maybe the luckiest guy on the eastern seaboard...no, make that the entire planet."

"How's that?" Julia teased him. "Is there a winning lottery ticket around here someplace you forgot to tell me about?"

"Who needs one of those? I've got the best ball club in the major leagues, lady."

"That sounds pretty lucky," Julia agreed.

"And even better than that," he said, his hands floating down over her back under the sheet and finally covering her bottom. "I've got the smartest, sexiest, most beautiful woman on earth in love with me. Now how do you figure all this good luck could happen to one guy?"

"I think you must be living right, Donovan," she said, staring down into his big, beautiful, unshaven face. Sometimes she felt as if she loved him so much, she couldn't even speak.

"Think so, huh?" he murmured as he pulled her head down for a kiss. Those were the last words they exchanged for a long time.

Julia was the first to finally get out of bed. She pulled on a huge Eagles' T-shirt that practically reached her knees. In Storm's compact kitchen, she located a frying pan and some eggs, then set about fixing them for breakfast. More like lunch, she amended, noticing the time.

While the coffee perked, Storm set the table, then went out to get his mail. He tossed his bills on the countertop, opting to read the newspaper, which he immediately opened to the sports section. With a dramatic delivery worthy of a Shakespearean actor, he read each article aloud that described the Eagles' big win.

Julia was pouring herself a second cup of coffee when she noticed Storm had gotten suddenly quiet. "Well? Go on—aren't there any more?" she prodded him.

"One more," he said, barely glancing up from the paper. "About you in fact."

"Me?" She sat down, carefully taking a sip of her coffee. "I didn't give anyone an interview."

"Looks like you didn't have to. Somebody talked their head off to this guy though. I'll be—he even knows your shoe size."

From the look on Storm's face, Julia guessed the article's tone was rather negative. She was touched by how upset Storm looked on her account. "Pretty bad, huh?"

"Depends on how you look at it," Storm answered tightly. "He says, and I quote, '. . . The amazing recovery of the Eagles would not have been possible without emergency resuscitation by the brilliant Dr. Archer. Not only has her sport psychology expertise put hitters like MacDougal back in action, but her behind-the-scenes management skills have proven invaluable—'" Storm's voice rose slightly and Julia winced. "Oh, by the way, the title of this literary masterpiece is, 'Just What The Doctor Orders'—"

"Stop, Storm. I can read it to myself." She reached for the paper but he snatched it out of her grasp.

"No, let me finish. It gets better," he promised. "'Donovan must have tossed his computer into the garbage when the good doctor came along. Surely she's been the real brains behind his throne these past few weeks. There can be no other explanation for this major-league, medical miracle.'"

"I get the idea," Julia said, jumping up and taking the paper out of his hands. Finally he let her see it.

"Careful now, you'll rip it. I really want to save that one for my scrapbook."

Julia looked down at the column, then back up at Storm. She didn't know what to say. How could they have been so deliriously happy seconds ago and so miserable right now?

"I know it's bad, but in a few days no one will remember. It's only the *Tribune*, not the *New York Times*," she said, trying to find an up side.

"This guy's trash is in the *Times*. It's a nationally syndicated column. I bet he's in more newspapers than 'Dear Abby'."

"I know you're upset. But no one is going to believe that. Everyone on the club knows it's not true."

"You'd be amazed how many people believe what they read in the papers, Julia. Even guys who've been playing for me for years. Don't think it's going to stop here. Reporters are going to be after everyone on the team now, digging for more dirt."

"I'm going to call up the newspaper," she said, heading for the telephone. "I'll have them print a retraction. I'll threaten to sue," she insisted, checking the newspaper's masthead for a telephone number.

"No—don't do that," Storm said. He took the receiver out of her hand and hung it back up. "It might be throwing oil on the fire. When we get to the stadium we'll speak to the PR department. Maybe they can put together some kind of statement."

Storm ran his hand through his already disheveled hair, then sat down heavily in a kitchen chair. Julia stood behind him and put her hands on his shoulders. Sometimes she couldn't wait until the baseball season was over. Win, lose or draw, she wanted Storm all to herself. She was tired of riding this crazy roller coaster called major-league baseball. Storm was really taking this last dip hard. She hated to see him so upset.

"Don't worry," she whispered, rubbing his shoulders. "You've got better things to think about. Your team chased the Lions out of town last night, remember?"

"Don't you understand, Julia? How can I run a ball club if my players don't respect me? Who gave that guy his information? It had to be somebody close to the team, Tucker, or Belcher maybe," he said glumly, wondering out loud who had betrayed him.

"Are you kidding? Those guys would never do something like that to you. They're your friends. They think the world of you."

"I don't know what to think right now," he said. He looked at his watch. "Damn—look at the time. Granville called a meeting in his office for two o'clock."

With the team in first place and only one week left of regular-season play, Charlie thought it was time to start discussing strategy for the play-off games, where the Eagles would most likely meet the Los Angeles Dodgers.

"I'm supposed to be there too, remember?" Julia asked him as he dashed back into the bathroom again.

"Oh—right," he said, as he began to lather his face with shaving cream. "Well, you sure can't go up there dressed like that, honey," he said, referring to her scanty attire. "Unless you're shooting for the front page today—"

"I'm going back to the hotel to change. I'll see you later," she said. She kissed an unlathered cheek, then went into the bedroom to put on her clothes from the day before.

Arriving at her hotel, Julia drove into the underground lot and parked. She felt silly putting on sunglasses just to get from her car to the elevator, then up to her room. But she suddenly felt as though nosy reporters were hiding in every corner, ready to pop out at her and cause even more trouble.

When she reached the building where Granville's office was, she found out that her fears were not unfounded. As she looked for the right elevator bank, two reporters stopped her, firing questions at her with both barrels.

"I really don't have time to talk to you now," Julia said, sidestepping them like a quarterback eluding a tackle. When the elevator door opened she jumped aboard, not even aware of where it was going.

Some time after an elevator tour of Granville's building, Julia finally walked into the meeting room. Charlie greeted her warmly. Storm and the other coaches were already there, including some executives from the team's front office whom Julia had only met once or twice.

She took a seat at the end of the long table. Hardly anybody looked at her. Not even Storm. Something told her they'd been discussing the newspaper article before she had entered. In fact, she spotted a neatly clipped copy of the piece lying in front of Charlie at the head of the table.

Julia decided that for Storm's sake, and her own, she would only speak when she was spoken to today. Until the smoke cleared and Storm calmed down, she could keep her opinions to herself. If something really crucial came up, she could always speak to Storm about it privately.

But despite Julia's good intentions, the tide of the conversation went from bad to worse. On almost every issue, she heard one of the coaches ask, "Well, what does Julia think about it?" Or, "Julia would know if he could hold up under that kind of pressure. What does she say?"

She tried to deflect these questions toward Storm, without being too obvious about it. But she could see that her attempts at diplomacy were getting him even angrier. Again and again, it seemed that her assessment of situations was more sought after than Storm's.

Finally, while Storm was explaining why he chose to platoon Valentine and Russo at third base, instead of making one of them the permanent shortstop, a vice-president from the front office cut him off in midsentence.

"Maybe we should hear from Dr. Archer regarding this," he said.

Julia couldn't speak. Her gaze was fixed on Storm. She had never seen him so angry before.

"That's it! I've had it!" Storm threw up his hands and got out of his chair. "You want Dr. Archer's opinion, you can have it. You can have her on a silver platter," he said, turning to give Julia a look that cut straight to her heart. "Let her be your manager for the rest of the season," he said. "I quit!"

He turned, then left the meeting room, slamming the door behind him. The room was completely silent. Charlie tapped his legal pad with the tip of his gold pen. Then, through the closed door they heard a crash and the receptionist's cry of alarm. "Mr. Donovan!" she said. Another door slammed, then it was quiet again.

"Five'll get you ten it was the watercooler," Eddie whispered to Julia.

"I think that was enough for today, gentlemen," Charlie said smoothly, adjourning the meeting. "Thank you for coming."

The men got up, then slowly began to file out of the meeting room, talking quietly to each other about the grand finale, Julia suspected. She purposely lingered behind the group; she gathered her composure as she walked up to Charlie.

"May I speak to you in private?" she asked him.

"Of course, Julia. Let's go into my office." They walked through a door from the meeting room directly into Charlie's office. He offered her a seat, the same one she'd sat in the first time they met, she recalled.

"If this is about Storm, you needn't worry. You don't really think I accepted that high melodrama as an actual resignation, do you?"

"I didn't think so," she said honestly.

"He'll be over this newspaper fiasco in a day or so. On to something else to blow his top over by then—"

"I don't think so," Julia said. "This is serious to him. He feels like everyone's lost confidence in him."

"Who's lost confidence in him? I sure as hell haven't, after all, I'm paying his salary. Doesn't that count for something?"

"I'm referring to the players. The coaches—" Julia felt very upset, almost overwhelmed when she considered how messy this situation had become. Maybe she shouldn't have persisted with the Eagles. Perhaps Storm had been right from the start. Too many cooks spoil the broth and all that. "You have to consider it from his side."

"It's easier for you, dear," Charlie said calmly. "Because you're in love with him, I mean. Don't look so shocked." Charlie laughed. "I've known for weeks.

Ever since you two had dinner with me after I returned from the Orient."

"Then you knew well before I did," Julia said finally. He laughed. "Now you'll understand why I have to resign," she added.

"What do you mean? We need you now more than ever. First Donovan gets hysterical on me, now you. It must be something in the air today," he told her.

"Charlie, I'm serious," she said. "My job is done. There's no sense in my hanging around. It'll only cause more trouble for Storm."

"You've got a contract, you know," Charlie said. "I could hold you to it. Sue you. Are you willing to take that chance?"

"Yes—yes, I am." She looked him straight in the eye. "Everyone's so eager to hear my advice about the Eagles all of a sudden? Well, here it is, I think the best thing for the club's morale and the concentration of their excitable manager would be for Dr. Archer to step out of the picture right now, so they could play some pure-and-simple baseball."

Charlie looked down at her, releasing a weary sigh. She could tell he had given up arguing with her about it. "I'm not nullifying that contract," he said. "You'll still get your bonuses if the team wins the play-offs and the World Series—"

"You don't have to do that," Julia cut in.

"Nonsense. You deserve it. And more." He took her hand, enfolding it in both of his. "This isn't goodbye, Julia."

"I hope not," she said. "I know the team will go all the way."

"Oh sure thing...but I wonder if they'll let me watch it in the hospital," he said musingly.

"The hospital? Is something wrong?" She searched his face to see if he was joking with her again.

"Not yet, but if the rest of the week is anything like today, I'm going to have a nervous breakdown."

With Charlie's best wishes, Julia left. The afternoon crowd, returning from lunch, helped her avoid any lingering reporters in the lobby. She took a cab back to her hotel and once again sneaked up to her room feeling like either an undercover agent, or an escaped criminal. Her gaze immediately went to the message light on her phone, but it wasn't flashing. Storm had not called her.

He probably expected her to come down to the stadium. She wondered what she should do. She knew he was upset, but her feelings were hurt, too. After all, this wasn't all her fault. When he'd burst out with his "silver platter" line, she'd felt he was sending her a private message, that he was finished with their private relationship as well.

She had believed he really loved her. But maybe it wasn't so. Maybe their long shot really hadn't come in. Working together so closely gave their relationship the illusion of real love. But as soon as they hit a rough spot, Storm's true colors showed through.

Baseball was his first and only true love, she thought. Hadn't he told her that once? She couldn't mean that much to him if he was so willing to put the Eagles above everything, above his feelings for her. Julia grabbed a handful of tissues and wiped her eyes. If she wasn't so sad she would be laughing at the fact that after all, it was Storm who turned out to be the pragmatic one. It was a silly dream to think that two complete opposites could ever have made things work. That only happens in the movies, she reminded herself.

# Ten

As Julia waited at the gate for her flight to San Diego, she half expected Storm to appear and convince her to stay, as he had once before. She even wore her sunglasses, once again to hide her puffy eyes. But of course, he never showed. She boarded the plane, feeling foolish for even entertaining the notion that Storm would be sorry that she'd gone. Two was company, three was a crowd. Far be it from her to come between him and his only love—his precious baseball team.

Back in San Diego, she had a truckload of mail to sort through, much of it requesting her consulting services. Her success with the Eagles had certainly advanced her reputation. But Julia only saw the pile of mail as a good way to distract herself for the next few weeks, while she tried to get over Storm.

During her time with the Eagles, she had studiously taken down pages and pages of notes—her observations about the team's morale and a million and one juicy tidbits that would help her support her theories about team psychology and group motivation. Perhaps her journal of her wild ride with the Eagles would even provide enough material for a book. It had seemed so important to her when she'd taken the job. But beating someone else in her field to the punch with these theories hardly seemed that crucial now. Julia didn't have the heart to even open the first notebook. She stacked it all on a shelf in her office, wondering how long it would take her to be able to return to it.

After taking a few days to settle in at home, she drove up the coast to visit one of her older brothers, his wife and children in San Francisco. They were happy to see her. Spending time with her family, especially her niece and nephew, cheered her up considerably. But it didn't take long before Julia's sister-in-law started asking questions. She knew that Julia's usual high spirits hadn't sunk so low just because of too much work. But Julia wasn't ready yet to talk about Storm.

When it was time for the Eagles to meet the Dodgers in the National League play-off games, Julia unplugged the TV. She would toss the sport section of the newspaper directly into the garbage every morning without looking at it. However, she couldn't help but hear snatches of news on the radio, or in conversation with her friends and colleagues. Like it or not, she was forced to keep apprised of the team's progress. The night they won the National League Pennant, she was irresistibly drawn to her TV. Like a woman possessed, she tuned in just in time to see live coverage from the clubhouse of their victory celebration.

There they were, in all their glory—Firecracker, Gonzalez, Eddie and Osgood, dancing around the locker room, spraying champagne on one another. Julia felt as if she were almost there with them. When Storm came into view, her heart nearly stopped beating. He looked exhausted; his face was drawn; he had dark rings under his eyes. A sportscaster was interviewing him, but Julia didn't hear a word. Her eyes feasted on the sight of him. Then, in the flash of an eye, he was gone. In the flash of an eye, she was staring wistfully at a tire commercial.

Storm had tried to speak to her after her abrupt departure from Boston. He'd left message after message on her machine, but she wouldn't answer any of his calls. He'd even sent her a letter. It wasn't a five-page apology, or a ten-page avowal of his love. Just a hastily dashed-off message that read, "You're being ridiculous. We need to talk. Pick up your phone!"

Julia decided it was best not to answer him. It wasn't going to lead anywhere. And pretty soon, Storm had given up trying to reach her. So she was right after all. Cold comfort indeed. Their passion for each other had brought them together, but it would never pull them through for the long haul. Determined to put it behind her, she forced herself to practice all kinds of fall-out-of-love exercises. For instance, every time she thought of Storm, she pictured him with Donald Duck's head on his shoulders, quacking away at an umpire. It didn't seem to work very well.

The phone rang, breaking into her thoughts. She picked up, surprised to hear a familiar male voice on the line. A few familiar male voices in fact. "We did it! We made it! Hey, Julia? You there? Guess who this is . . ."

"I'm here," she yelled back. "Congratulations! I was just watching you on TV—" It sounded as if half the team were huddled around the receiver, all trying to talk to her at once. "I knew you guys could do it."

The rest of the crazy conversation went much the same way. Ernie and Willie Tucker got on the line, too. She wondered if she was going to hear Storm's voice next. But then Ernie said he had to go and the line was silent.

Julia felt a bittersweet sense of satisfaction knowing she had been part of the club's success. It was touching to know that they hadn't forgotten about her tonight. But underneath it all, her soul still longed for Storm.

When the World Series began a few days later, Julia again tried her best to avoid baseball news like poison. The Eagles were matched against the Oakland Athletics and the winner of four out of seven won it all. The first two games were in Boston. The experts favored the Eagles to beat the Athletics, especially with the home-field advantage working for them.

Yet, for some mysterious reason Boston fell apart and lost the first game by a score of 6-0. When Julia happened to hear the news on her car radio, she decided to break down and read the newspaper's play-by-play account of the game. The merciless headline on the sport section read, "Eagles Lay An Egg." The reporter speculated that they had simply cracked under the pressure. Their defense was of Little League caliber, he observed; their offense was virtually non-existent.

Julia felt upset, but there was nothing she could do. She felt certain, however, that the Boston Eagles would come through smashingly. But the next game meant more bad news for Boston. Another bumbling effort, with the final score 7-2. The headline in her morning paper read, "Eagles Headed For Extinction?" Julia certainly hoped not. She read that they were flying to California that day for the next three games, the first of which would start tomorrow night. Oakland was already halfway there, needing only two more wins to end it.

Julia felt an unwelcome tug at her heart, knowing Storm would soon be so close, yet so far. She felt so powerless. Throughout the day, she wondered what she could do to help. Should she call to try to boost their spirits? No matter what had happened with Storm, she couldn't really let the club go down without hearing a word from her.

When she got home from her office that evening, she walked up to her front porch to find Storm sitting on the steps, waiting for her. He was reading a newspaper, the sport section of course. She stopped halfway up the walk, not quite believing that it was he. But he looked far too real and worn out to be a mirage.

"Just dropped by to deliver your newspaper," he said, holding out his travel-worn copy. His gaze took her in hungrily, from head to toe.

"Thanks—but we get the same news here," she said, finally feeling brave enough to step forward. "Why aren't you up in Oakland?"

"Guess I made a wrong turn on the freeway." He shrugged. "Those maps they give you with the rental cars are really a joke."

"Storm—" She didn't know what to say. He looked so tired. She wanted to sit down next to him, put her arms around him and pretend that everything was perfect again between them. But it wasn't. "Why don't you come inside?" she said finally, walking past him to open the door.

"Thanks—" He got up to follow her. They walked into the living room, but remained standing. "That painting looks like I feel," he said, passing the big abstract he had once pretended to admire.

"That bad, huh?" Julia had to smile. God, she'd missed his silly jokes, missed everything about him. Just being in the same room with him again was like some kind of miracle.

"Almost, but not quite." He sighed as his gaze rested on her. He ran his hand through his mussed hair. "Which brings me to the reason I'm here, care to go one last round of Let's Make a Deal?"

"I don't think so—no," she said, crossing her hands over her chest. "Our wheeling-and-dealing days are over, Storm."

"Just a second—" he implored her. "You haven't heard what's behind the curtain yet, Doc—"

From the look in his eyes and the way he said that silly nickname, her resistance broke down. She sat down at the corner of the couch, her legs curled beneath her. "Go ahead. You drove pretty far for this, I guess."

"Okay, here's the deal." He sat down next to her on the couch, so close she could have reached out and touched him. She had to force herself not to. "All you have to do is give me some of your special visualization exercises. In fact, even if you just let me look at you a while, instead of me picturing you constantly in my mind, that would be okay, too." He glanced at her briefly, to check her reaction, then continued. "My right brain and left brain seem to be on the disabled list lately, Doctor. Which should be no surprise to anyone since most of the time I act like I've got no brains at all."

"That's not true," she said softly. He reached over, took her hand, then pressed it to his lips. She felt her eyes fill with tears.

"Yes it is," he replied. "I didn't cherish and protect the one thing in the world that matters to me the most, Julia. You. What we had together. All the plans I had for us—"

This was news to Julia. She knew he had plenty of plans for his ball club. But if Storm had given any thought to their future, he'd kept it a carefully guarded secret.

"I never knew you thought much about the future—ours, I mean," Julia admitted. "Not beyond the next road trip, anyway."

"Of course I did. All the time. Even more since you left," he said. "It's not the players' fault they've been losing. It's me. I'm either biting their heads off, or brooding. I'm like an orchestra conductor who's giving the musicians all the wrong signals. The bottom line is, I really don't care anymore if the club wins the World Series—"

"You don't?" Julia had thought he'd come to ask her help. Had he really only come because he wanted them to be together again?

"What's another ball game?" He shrugged.

"We're talking about the Eagles winning the World Series," she reminded him, not quite believing what she'd heard.

"And I'm talking about you and me, Julia. About our future. That's what I've come here to talk about. You give me you, and I'll give you me. That's my deal," he said, moving closer to put his arms around her. "Will you marry me?"

"Wha-? Yes—" she said, right before he kissed her. Julia's head was spinning. She felt like a hurricane had just swept into her living room. Of course she wanted to marry him. The man really did have a few screws loose if he didn't know the answer to that question.

"Let's get married right away. Tonight—" Storm whispered against her mouth. He held her so tightly she could hardly answer. "I love you so much—"

"And I love you...Francis," she said, deciding that if ever there was a time to call Storm by his real name, this had to be it. Julia fell back on the couch with Storm's arms around her. Wrapped in a loving embrace, their hands and lips and sweet sighs of desire expressed their need for each other where words had left off.

Julia had never taken a shower in champagne and she had rarely been interviewed by network TV reporters. But the night the Eagles won the World Series in Boston, she enjoyed both experiences with Storm by her side.

After losing the first two games of the series, the Eagles had battled back to win four, earning themselves the title of World Champions. Except for cheering until her throat was sore, she'd hardly offered a word of professional advice. It wasn't necessary. After she and Storm were married, they hurried back to Oakland. He bounded into action like a general taking charge of a battlefield. He was back to his familiar, fiery, headstrong self again and the Eagles were galvanized back into action.

While the team celebrated wildly out in the locker room, a slightly more sedate group met in Storm's office.

"I'd like to use glasses if you two don't mind," Charles Granville said, filling Storm's and Julia's glasses with champagne. "Here's to one hell of a season," he said heartily, touching their glasses with his own. "And to next season—"

"Hear, hear!" Storm chimed in.

"Next season?" Julia met her husband's gaze, feeling the champagne take a wrong turn in her throat.

"No National League team has ever won the pennant and World Series two years in a row, honey," he pointed out to her.

"How interesting," Julia said blandly. Seeing the look on her face, Storm burst out laughing. He put his arm around her, giving her a tight hug.

"But first things first, Charlie," he said, raising his glass. "Here's a toast to my wife, my best friend, my true love—" He paused to look into Julia's eyes. "I don't know where I'd be without her.... But I don't plan to ever find out."

"I'll drink to that," Julia said, giving her husband a smile. She knew that this season was only the start of a lifetime of loving, laughing and arguing out the "tough calls" with Storm.

\*   \*   \*   \*   \*

 **Silhouette Desire**®

# COMING
# NEXT MONTH

**#517 BEGINNER'S LUCK—Dixie Browning**
Meet September's *Man of the Month*, Clement Barto. Mating habits:
unexplored. Women scared him speechless—literally. But with a little
beginner's luck, Clem was about to discover something called love....

**#518 THE IDEAL MAN—Naomi Horton**
Corporate headhunter Dani Ross had to find the right man for a client—
but the job title was "Husband." When she met rancher Jake Montana
she knew he was ideal—for her!

**#519 ADAM'S WAY—Cathie Linz**
Business efficiency expert Julia Trent insisted on a purely professional
relationship with problem-solver Adam MacKenzie. But he was
determined to make her see things Adam's way.

**#520 ONCE IN LOVE WITH JESSIE—Sally Goldenbaum**
Who says opposites don't attract? Confirmed bachelor Matt Ridgefield
had been content with his solitary life-style before carefree, spirited Jessie
Sager had come along. The professor had a lot to learn!

**#521 ONE TOUCH OF MOONDUST—Sherryl Woods**
Paul Reed was the most *romantic* man Gabrielle Clayton had ever met. He
was also her new roommate—and suddenly practical Gaby was dreaming
of moonlight and magic.

**#522 A LIVING LEGEND—Nancy Martin**
Hot on the trail of the scoop of the century, Catty Sinclair found only
gruff recluse Seth Bernstein. What *was* this gorgeous man doing in the
middle of nowhere...?

---

# AVAILABLE NOW:

You'll flip . . . your pages won't!
Read paperbacks *hands-free* with

# Book Mate · I

**The perfect "mate" for all your romance paperbacks**

**Traveling • Vacationing • At Work • In Bed • Studying
• Cooking • Eating**

Perfect size for all standard paperbacks, this wonderful invention makes reading a pure pleasure! Ingenious design holds paperback books OPEN and FLAT so even wind can't ruffle pages — leaves your hands free to do other things. Reinforced, wipe-clean vinyl-covered holder flexes to let you turn pages without undoing the strap . . . supports paperbacks so well, they have the strength of hardcovers!

Pages turn WITHOUT opening the strap

SEE-THROUGH STRAP

Reinforced back stays flat

Built in bookmark

BOOK MARK

BACK COVER HOLDING STRIP

10 x 7¼ opened
Snaps closed for easy carrying, too